WHITE SAND COCOON

A COLLECTION OF PRIZEWINNING SHORT STORIES

JO DERRICK

ISBN 978-1-9993014-0-8

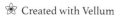 Created with Vellum

To Nige, Matt and Megan
For their unstinting love and support

CONTENTS

1

THE BLACK QUEEN

He has been carrying the chess piece around in the pocket of his checked shorts for most of the day. Billy knows it will give him power; make him strong. It will prepare him for what is to come.

He grabs a thistle flower on the verge, expecting it to bite and wound, but instead its fronds are soft. This isn't the first surprise he's experienced today.

Earlier, after he'd stolen an apple from Mrs Maddox's tree, Billy found a bunch of fresh flowers tied to the old oak where the road bends sharply to descend to the beach. He didn't know what the flowers were called, but they were mostly pink and white. Really pretty, they were and he knew they'd be perfect for Lisa. He owed her a present and a whisker of kindness, after he'd accidentally made her leg bleed this morning. He still wasn't a very good shot with his homemade catapult.

"You can stuff your flowers, Billy Sexton," she told him and slammed the door in his face.

Billy was surprised to feel the sting of tears. Lisa was stroppy for a ten-year-old. She was in the year below him at school and he'd had a soft spot for her ever since she'd shared her rhubarb and custard sweets with him one Thursday morning. He saw himself as her protector and made sure those bullies, Gina Shaw and Deborah Rowe didn't get anywhere near her. Lisa didn't show any gratitude, but he supposed that was girls for you.

He dropped the flowers on Lisa's front doorstep and wandered off towards the woods at the top end of the village.

His mates, Malcy and Sean, haven't shown up today. Billy trails his nail-bitten fingers through the dry brown stalks of cow parsley and wishes he had someone to play with. He fancies rolling down the sand dunes or skimming stones in the sea, but neither of those things are much fun when you're on your own.

He plunges his hand into the pocket of his shorts again. The Black Queen is still there; her hard, knobbly shape reassuring. Her blackness smoulders like coal. He wanted to show her to Lisa earlier and a streak of disappointment slices through him once again.

Lisa.

"If you give me a £10 note, I'll show you my knickers," she'd told him the other day.

As if he could pluck that much money out of thin air! He'd looked inside his mum's purse, but when he opened it out, there was only a fiver, and a few coppers in the zipped up bit. Then he remembered his ma had spent a tenner on hair dye, because Tosspot Terry said he preferred women with jet black hair.

Looked like it would be beans on toast for tea for the rest of the week. She'd been to The Flying Horse two nights running and hadn't even won on the Bingo. Tosspot Terry had stayed over both of those nights and Billy saw him help himself to the 'rainy day' money in the Cadbury's biscuit tin when he thought no one was looking.

It's getting late and Billy sits on the hill behind the park to watch the sun going down. He doesn't wear a watch, but he knows that once the sun has set, his mum will be in a good mood and there'll be a few empty Carlsberg cans on the kitchen worktop. She might even let him go to the chippy, if she can find enough coppers to make a quid. A bag of chips beat beans on toast any day, especially when his mum used those Lidl own label beans which cost about 15p.

The sky looks bruised even though it's lit up with a sheen of burnished gold, the colour of the shield he'd made for their Boudicca exhibition at school. He wishes Lisa was sat beside him. He'd hold her hand and tell her that God had used a gold-tinged brush and dipped it into raspberry pink paint. She likes it when he talks like that. He can't understand why she was in such a bad mood today. Sean and Malcy warned him that girls got temperamental and tearful when they got to ten. They both had sisters, so they should know.

Billy shivers. It's cold now the sun's gone to bed and he's wearing the Sonic T-shirt, which has worn thin with too many washes. If he runs home, it will warm him up.

As he slices through the long grass at the bottom of the hill, he feels happier than he has all day. It's only when he gets to the corner of his street, that he realises the black queen chess piece is no longer in his pocket.

He leans against the street sign, out of breath and close to tears. He can't lose her. She's the most powerful piece in the set and she'll make him strong. He can't face Tosspot Terry or his mum without her. He'll have to go back.

It's getting dark and as the streetlights come on,

Billy realises how hungry he is. He passes the steamed-up fug of the chip shop; the smell of golden batter and fresh fish creeping into his nostrils like the sea-urchin fronds of the thistle flowers. He lingers for a moment, wondering whether Old Maggie behind the counter will take pity on him and give him a paper bag of scrumps. Those golden pieces of leftover batter are better than anything he's ever tasted when he gets them for free, but Maggie isn't behind the counter today. It's a young girl with greasy black hair and a scowl on her face.

He makes his way up the hill and tries to retrace his steps. He can just about make out the flattened grass and gets down on his hands and knees. As he crawls, Billy pretends he's a member of a police search team, going over every inch of the field looking for evidence. He has to find the Black Queen. Things will never be the same if she is lost for good.

He pats his hands on the ground feeling for the familiar lump of heavy plastic. His granda would never forgive him if he's lost it. His set will be ruined. He can picture Granda shaking his fist from heaven and cursing him the way he did when he broke Granda's favourite Patsy Cline record by accident that time.

Billy tastes his tears, which he no longer has the power to stop. By the time he reaches the top of the hill, it's pitch black and he's sobbing. Does he turn back for home or does he carry on looking? If he waits till the morning, then some other kid might nab the chess piece and claim it for their own. His ma is probably in The Flying Horse already, smoking her Benson and Hedge's with a pint of lager and black on the table in front of her. Tosspot Terry will be playing pool or feeding the jukebox with pound coins. Billy will have to get his own tea. There won't be any chips tonight.

Billy walks slowly back down the hill, the shrubs and brambles looming up out of the darkness like monsters. Billy automatically feels in his pocket for the chess piece. The Black Queen will make him strong. He's never scared when she's around, but she's not there.

As he passes Lisa's house, he hears a hiss and a whisper.

"Billy! Round the back!"

He can't see her, but tip-toes around the side of her house like a cat burglar, glad of his plimsolls, which don't make a sound on the crazy-paving path. A white twisted snake slithers down the wall from one of the upstairs windows. It's not until he gets closer that he realises what it is. Sheets twisted and knotted like Rapunzel's plait. A leg appears from out of the window, and Lisa begins to climb down, her skinny legs gripping the makeshift rope with a confidence that tells him she's done this many times before.

When she reaches the bottom, she grasps his cheeks and kisses him on the lips.

"Come on, Billy. We're going on an adventure."

Lisa seems so much older than him, as she leads him into the dark street illuminated only by pools of artificial light. Her mood is the opposite of what it was earlier.

"I've got grub and some pop," she says, patting the rucksack on her back. "I'll take you to my den in the woods. Ever spent the night outdoors, Billy?"

He hasn't. Not really. The time Ma locked him out by accident didn't count.

They head up the field with the long grass, retracing his earlier steps back up the hill towards the wood.

"My girl," whispers Billy with pride. Who needed The Black Queen when he had Lisa?

They set up camp in the heart of the wood, listening to a lone owl hooting in the distance and the scuffle of tiny creatures in the undergrowth.

"Scared Billy?" Lisa asks, laying an old woollen blanket on the ground. "You look scared."

He shakes his head and takes the bag of crisps she offers him. They're Walkers Cheese n' Onion, not the cheap rubbishy ones his mum buys from Lidl.

He scoffs them down almost without tasting them. He reaches for the Lyons cake in a blue box, Lisa has just placed on the ground. The smell of chocolate mingles with the earthy scents of woodland floor.

"Can I?" he asks.

"You ain't had no tea, have you, Billy?"

He shakes his head, shoveling in handfuls of cake. It feels like he hasn't eaten in weeks. Crumbs tumble down the front of his T-shirt and Lisa brushes them away with a flick of her hand.

"Steady on. You'll be sick," she says, her voice full of concern.

Who needs The Black Queen when you have someone like Lisa to take care of you? Billy suddenly feels the urge to tell Lisa about the lost chess piece, but just as he's about to speak, an arc of blue light spins its way up the hill to their camp.

"Coppers!" shrieks Lisa. "They're looking for us already."

Billy's stomach flips and flaps like a landed fish. He feels sick. He tries hard not to be, but within seconds he's vomiting up the cake and the crisps next to a nearby tree.

He can hear Lisa tut before she starts clearing up the remains of their picnic. He didn't even have any pop and now he's thirsty, but daren't ask her for some.

They watch the twinkly lights of the village below and

then hear shouts and whistles. Dogs barking from the bottom of the hill.

"They're searching for us," Lisa whispers, her voice full of excitement and awe.

Billy holds onto his stomach and wishes he'd ignored Lisa earlier and gone home instead. Perhaps the real police search team will find his chess piece?

"Come on, Billy," says Lisa quietly packing up. "We'll go round the back of the wood and home. We can't stay now."

He stands up, feeling a sense of relief wash over him like soft, foamy waves on a hot day. He feels about three-years-old as Lisa takes him by the hand and leads him through the wood, then down the field of stubble, away from the police and the dogs.

He wishes he'd been able to share the sunset with her earlier. He'd have felt more grown-up then.

They go to Billy's house first. There aren't any lights on and he lets himself in. Lisa gives him a peck on the cheek in the doorway and runs off back to hers.

Still feeling sick, Billy goes straight to bed and lies awake for hours thinking about how the police will find his chess piece and that he'll never get it back now.

BRIGHT SUNLIGHT WAKES HIM, blasting through his ripped curtains like a laser. Something doesn't feel right and Billy listens for the usual early morning sounds of Tosspot Terry coughing his guts up in the bathroom and the clatter of dishes in the kitchen.

Silence.

The bed sheets are twisted around his legs like ropes,

and Billy remembers Lisa's escape from her bedroom window the night before.

Even as he creeps downstairs, Billy knows there's no one else is in the house.

The first thing he sees when he enters the kitchen is a £10 note on the table, propped up against a plastic bottle of Daddies Sauce, its top crusted with dried rings of brown. There's a note.

Won on the lottery, son. Treat y'self to chippy supper. Gone to Flying Horse. Mum.

The first thing Billy thinks about as he holds the note, is giving it to Lisa so that she'll show him her knickers. Maybe she'd have shown him for free last night, if the police hadn't come looking for them.

So where is his ma now?

Billy holds the tenner in his hand and looks around the kitchen. He'll go to the shop and buy lots of crisps and some chocolate for breakfast, then he'll go and look for the chess piece again. The Black Queen will make him strong enough to look for Ma.

He's just about to open the front door when there's a knock. He opens it to a policewoman and a lady in a smart suit.

"Can we come in, Billy, love? It's about your mum," the policewoman says.

Billy shoves the £10 note deep into his pocket. It doesn't have the same power as The Black Queen and he feels tears pricking his eyes. He thinks about the bunch of pink and white flowers he left for Lisa yesterday and wishes he'd given them to his ma instead.

≈

LATER, when they lead him to the car, they take the black bin liner from him and put it in the boot. All the stuff he has is in there. Everything apart from the black queen chess piece, which is why he's in this mess now. If he hadn't lost The Black Queen, then everything would be the same as normal and he'd have his power back.

He looks down at the road. The tar is melting already. It's going to be a scorcher, as his granda used to say.

As they drive out of the village, Billy looks at the field of long grass leading up the hill; the police crime tape fluttering in the whisper-quiet breeze. He pictures his Black Queen lying there abandoned and the soft pink fronds of the thistle flowers gently stroking her face.

2

THE FLEDGLING

Pewter clouds billow on the horizon, spliced with red bands of setting sun. I'm doing a steady 50mph and I sense that Sean is restless. I'm driving him to The Box Factory. A certain irony in the name. I don't want to do this, but it's what Sean wants and at the end of the day, that is what matters.

"All right?" I ask him, risking a glance in his direction. He looks shrunken in the passenger seat; a husk, as if he's shed several layers of skin. He's like a baby bird without feathers, too exposed and vulnerable to leave the nest.

"I'm fine. Bit nervous. In a few months time I'll be a regular and all will be well. Should have passed my test by then, too."

That's typical of Sean. So pragmatic. I wish I'd been more like him at his age. I was a late developer, you see.

There's a queue outside The Box Factory, an old build-ing; used to be a mechanical engineers' institute or some-thing. I expect it looks grander on the outside than the inside. I can't imagine what the interior will look like. Bright red walls? Lots of pink? Lots of men, that's for sure.

Probably all older than Sean. I picture The Village People; hulks with black moustaches and tight jeans. Someone dressed as an American cop. A George Michael look-a-like or two.

I drop him down the street.

"Have a good night, Sean. Be careful. I'll pick you up here at 12, okay?"

He nods and slams the passenger door shut. My heart sinks and I collapse into the driver's seat with a sense of relief. I've done it. I've crossed another boundary. I feel almost euphoric and give myself a pat on the back.

Do I really want to drive back home yet? Then the fifteen mile journey back here. Shirley will understand if I text her to say I'll wait it out in a nearby café.

It takes a while to find somewhere to park. The café is rather dull. Chipped heavy mugs with tea stains. Workmen sit at the table opposite discussing who they fancied most in the Celebrity Big Brother house. Shirley will be watching that back at home; her feet up with a glass of Shiraz. I suddenly feel homesick and wish I'd driven back.

"Mind if I join you?"

A thirty-something guy plonks himself down before I have chance to answer.

"Dropped your kid off at a gig, I bet," he says, stirring his coffee.

"Yes, sort of. How did you..."

"I recognise your type. No offence. The NIA, is it? Great band on tonight, Wish I'd gone myself."

I don't know what to say. How can I tell this stranger that I've dropped my son at the most notorious gay club for miles for his first experience of nightlife in the big city? The only social life Sean is interested in. The places his friends frequent in our market town hold no interest for him.

They're all chasing girls and Sean is left sitting alone with a vodka shot and a guilty conscience.

"Nice little café, this," says the guy. "Always drop in before going to The Box Factory."

I almost spill my coffee. It wasn't obvious. I want to tell him that my boy is in there. My innocent boy, who is probably about to have his first sexual encounter. I want to plead with him to look after Sean. Make sure he's all right. Watch out for him.

As the man gets up to leave, I look at his tight black jeans and rather feminine-looking shirt. He lays a hand on my arm.

"Don't worry, mate. I'll keep an eye out."

I watch him leave and swallow the lump in my throat. I sit and stare at the magnolia wall until my coffee goes cold.

In my journal, I'll write, 'I was at the café in Wellington Street when I finally learned to let go.'

When I step out into the night, I look up at the stars munching up the darkness. How can something that looks so fragile and small be so vast, so bright and so visible?

I text Shirley. Our fledgling has flown.

3

SMILE FOR THE CAMERA

The song again.
The third tailor said, "You've seen nothing at all."
And he buried the needle point deep in the wall
On the Rhine, on the Rhine
He flew back and forth through the needle's eye.

THEN THE VOICE.

"STOP YOUR DAYDREAMING, BOY! LOOK SHARP!"

He stood to attention, his fists clenched tight. He held his breath.

"Arms out to the side. Straighter. Fingers spread."

She walked to the farthest corner of the room, watching him all the time. He wasn't allowed to move his arms.

"Straight out like an aeroplane!" she ordered.

She picked up her needle and looked as if she was about to continue with the tapestry she sewed each night.

She walked towards him.

"Let's see how straight you keep those arms now. Remember, boy, no flinching!"

She aimed the needle at his left eye.

Don't blink. Blinking not allowed.

She laughed and lowered the needle until it brushed his lower lip. He could feel tears pricking his eyes. Couldn't move. Couldn't blink. Couldn't tremble. Couldn't weaken.

Stab! He took a sharp intake of breath. He couldn't help it.

Stab again. This time in his arm pit and it took every ounce of courage and strength to keep his arm still.

She laughed again. "Good boy!"

She turned her back to him. It was over. Just a few more seconds and he could relax. He started to exhale.

Stab. She'd turned so quickly. Too quickly. His cheek this time. Stab, stab, stab. Quick little movements. His chest, his tummy, his thigh.

She stopped. Laughed. Started again. Arms straight. Don't blink. Don't cry. Don't tremble.

Finally he crumpled in a heap on the floor. She'd won. Again.

A WHOLE MORNING at Chellington Primary School wasn't Steve's idea of fun. He hated photographing the younger kids. They were fidgety and noisy. It was much harder to get them into a decent pose. The older girls, the ten and eleven-year-olds were easier. They were just getting to that stage where they were either shy or pretending they were the next Twiggy or Susan Shaw.

The headteacher, Mrs Leadbetter, was stalking up and down the school hall as he set up his equipment. The lighting was tricky due to the huge window down the bottom end and the rope ladders, climbing frames against the bare brick walls and hobby horse reminded him of sadistic gym teachers at his own school when he was younger. Trust bloody John Wentworth to give him this assignment. He knew how much he hated doing the primary schools and now the police were sniffing round 'cos he took those photos at Perrymount, the school the missing girl attended. Still, it was better than being stuck in the shop, demonstrating cameras to boring old gits.

The older kids were lined up outside now. The boys first. They were sulky and sullen, wearing hand-knitted jumpers in dull shades of mustard or pale blue. Only a few wore their hair longer and several had those basin cuts their mothers did for them, with a face full of fringe shading their eyes, which looked crap in the photo, because he couldn't get the light quite right. It was as bad as if they were wearing a hat. Trying to coax a smile out of the buggers was well nigh impossible. A bit of chat about football usually helped.

The girls were better. Some had budding breasts and burgeoning hips. Steve could tell straightaway which ones would be the lookers who could turn guys' heads in a few years time.

Take this one sitting on the box now. Taller than the rest of the girls; small breasts nudging her tight pink polo-necked sweater; long, dark shiny hair and a pretty face. Her mud brown eyes sparkled when he winked at her. She giggled and squirmed a little, and he took a couple of impromptu shots. Not for the school. No, he'd save these for himself.

"Okay, now smile for me, okay? This one's for your mum," he told her in his most commanding, professional voice.

That was better. More the sort of school photo her mother would expect.

There was only one other girl who was interesting. Very shy, looking at the floor most of the time, then when she did finally look up at the camera, she batted her long dark eyelashes. She had an elfin-like face and baby blonde hair. Too thin, for his tastes, but there was something about her.

He snapped away, taking several shots. Most he'd keep.

As he packed away his equipment, the dinner ladies began to put out the tables for lunch. School dinners. More unwelcome memories dived in from the past. Grisly mutton and cold pilchards in tomato sauce. Miss Batten, the head-mistress of Kipton School, long since retired, forcing him to eat every last morsel on his plate. Old Rubber Neck, they called her. A bit too fond of the cane and beating boys' back-sides with the flat of her hand. Steve shuddered, as he snapped the last case shut.

"Would you like to stay for some lunch, Mr Brindley?" Mrs Leadbetter asked. She seemed a kind woman and the sort of teacher that should be in charge of a primary school. Kids today didn't know how lucky they were.

"No, thanks. I'll pick up a sandwich on the way back to the shop. We should have the proofs back to you in the next couple of weeks."

"Lovely. I hope they all behaved themselves?"

Steve smiled. "Yeah, they're not a bad bunch. I've had a lot worse."

He followed her out through the offices and out of the swing doors to the car park. The weather had got colder the last couple of weeks.

It was only when he was driving back to Limeworth that he remembered he'd promised his mother he'd buy matches and candles in his lunch hour. Bugger! It was like finding a needle in a haystack.

Needles. No, don't think about needles, Steve.

He pressed his foot hard on the accelerator as he approached the main Limeworth Road. The Capri bucked a little and he corrected her. She wasn't great on handling, but that was all part of the fun.

The lights were out at Bell Corner again. Russian Roulette on one of the worst junctions in Limeworth. Why didn't they put a bobby on traffic duty? Probably all been drafted in to Saltley to sort the pickets out. What was the country coming to? It was more like 1932 rather than 1972.

Steve parked the Capri at the back of Tesco's and strolled through the precinct. A few Limeworth Grammar School girls were sitting on a bench eating huge cream buns, but red-haired Alison wasn't amongst them. He hadn't had chance to speak to her for a while. Now he'd extended his running route, he didn't often see her getting off the afternoon school bus. He wasn't sure what the best approach was. He didn't want to scare her off. Then there was the problem of finding a location for her to pose for him. The attics at Kipton Hall were ideal. He was used to breaking in there, but the memories of his childhood made it impossible to feel remotely comfortable there on his own. It would be different if someone was with him. Someone as vulnerable as he had once been.

He had to try five different shops before he found one that had candles left. His mother would kill him if he went home empty handed. She didn't drive and the village shop had run out ages ago.

Bloody miners!

Steve bought two boxes of plain white candles and a box of Swan Vesta. That would have to do. The power cuts were going to get longer, they said. The miners were stopping the lorries getting through to the coking depots now.

Still no sign of Alison. Maybe she'd caught an earlier bus or had a dental appointment or something.

Steve was just about to give up and go back to work, when he spotted Kate Marchant chatting to a guy outside Tamworth Joinery. Interesting. Was she shagging someone else? He wouldn't be surprised. Everyone in Kipton knew her marriage to Brian had been on the rocks since their little girl drowned and she was a very attractive woman. He wouldn't mind having a crack at her himself, if it wasn't for the things she did to him as a kid.

So, who was the guy? From this distance he did look a bit like Brian. There was something about the way he held himself.

Shit! Steve's stomach dipped and dived as if he were on a roller coaster ride. He felt as if he was going to throw up. It was him. Greg. He'd come back, just as he said he would, the bastard! Now all became clear. Very cosy, the two of them. So, Kate had kept in touch, had she?

Steve ducked into the doorway of the newsagents and watched as his nemesis walked away from Kate, head down before ducking into the shoe shop right opposite where Steve was standing.

Greg was closer than he thought and more dangerous. If Steve fucked up, then he was done for. He had to find Alison.

He'd drive back home to Kipton and go for a run to clear his head. He had to make sure he was in tip-top shape for the pram race in August. Another few months of hard training ahead of him. He might even squeeze in the odd charity run.

Steve was fitter than he thought. After running up

Coppice Lane and back, then doing a circuit of the village, he decided to run up the Radway to Kipton Hall. Five miles in total. Not bad, considering.

As he approached the Hall, the light was beginning to fade. It was at times like this that he wished he'd had his camera to hand. The sky was clamouring for attention; dark clouds scudding across the horizon weaving in and out of bands of raspberry pink and blood orange red.

Then he noticed the Electricity Board vans leaving the hall in a quiet procession. So, the rumours were true. Someone had finally bought the old place. Whoever it was must be mad. Kipton Hall had fallen into a bad state of repair since Dolly Reid had died. He felt a tightening in his chest. The memories from his childhood sliced through him like a machete. He decided to head back to the village.

A rabbit running through the undergrowth on the verge alongside shook Steve back to the present. Up ahead he saw the school bus pulling into the bus-stop. A gaggle of teenagers poured out onto the pavement.

Amongst them, Alison.

Pretty in a plump kind of way. Reddish hair, crinkly curls and freckles. She reminded him of one of the girls in those Pre-Raphaelite paintings. A word sprang to mind. Titian. Yes, that was a better way of describing the colour of her hair. It was longish and framed her face in an attractive way. He needed to gain her trust. Soften her up a bit with the old charm to get the right sort of poses he wanted when the time came. He wondered what she'd look like naked. Frosty pale skin. A smattering of freckles on her thighs, perhaps? A golden bush. As he got closer to her, he tried to penetrate the colour co-ordinated uniform to see what was underneath. Pert young breasts thrust out from her hand knitted blue jumper.

"Hi, Steve!" she called, then looked shyly away.

He raised his hand, aware of his sweaty T-shirt, brief running shorts and red face. Steve slowed to a walk, then turned back and looked at the rear view. She'd got a gorgeous arse. Just the right shape. He pictured her lying naked on her stomach; her hair spread out over her back, bum slightly raised.

Would she smile for camera? Or would she be afraid like the other one?

He ran up to her. Feeling daring. Taking a risk.

"Alison! Over here. I've got a little proposition for you."

LAUGHING LLAMAS AND A
SAXOPHONE

They were like a couple of laughing llamas. Do llamas laugh? Probably not, but sometimes they look as if they're cracking up at some joke. I go to the zoo to watch the llamas most Sundays. I take photographs and sit on the bench opposite their enclosure, eating ice cream and wondering what could have been, had Marshall stayed at Number 24.

The two women are walking away now. They've probably noticed I'm staring at them. One is wearing a fur coat, which is ludicrous in the middle of June. She's hunched over like a crone and I notice she has at least two sheets of toilet paper stuck to her shoe. Should I run over and tell her?

Before I have chance, a young woman sits down beside me and takes out a saxophone. I hope she's not going to play that thing here. The llamas won't like it. Why is the zoo full of crack-pots today?

She starts to play the solo from *Baker Street* and I shuffle along the bench, hoping she'll get the hint. A grey-haired man pushing a chocolate-smeared toddler in a buggy walks past, then stops and looks down at the floor, probably expecting to see an open case in which to collect coins. The young woman's instrument case is closed, however, just like her eyes. I compare her long brown eyelashes with those of the llamas, who seem to be enjoying her performance. She obviously has some kind of affinity with them.

"I usually play saxophone with Mr Mitchell, my old music teacher," the young woman tells me when she's finished playing. "I'm Deborah, by the way."

Deborah holds out her hand and I shake it, noticing that it is clammy and damp. How vile. I'm so pleased I'm wearing cotton gloves.

"Mr Mitchell has a swing band. We play in the band-stand in Coddicott Park sometimes. We played at a beer festival in Oxfordshire yesterday. I love the Cotswolds, don't you?"

I smile. It doesn't do to reply to these kind of people. That simply gives them licence to quiz you about why you've chosen to spend your Sunday afternoon alone at the zoo.

I keep schtum, hoping she'll take the hint and walk away.

Deborah busies herself putting the saxophone away. The woman in the fur coat walks past again and points at the llamas who are now looking decidedly depressed. I'm not surprised. *Baker Street* wouldn't be the song I'd choose to play on a cheerless Sunday afternoon. The fur coat lady still has toilet paper attached to her shoe. It reminds me of the long ivory train Princess Diana wore on her wedding day and I wonder how long the toilet paper has been there. Since she left home, perhaps? It looks decidedly like Velvet Cushion Cocoa Butter; the upmarket kind of toilet paper you most definitely don't find in public toilets at a zoo.

"You do know Gerry Rafferty is dead, don't you?" I ask Deborah, who is taking a drink of water from one of those common plastic bottles that seem to be all the rage.

She looks confused for a moment.

"Erm, yes, of course. I used to be married to his cousin," she tells me.

It's a lie. It has to be. She's far too young to have been married to anyone.

"I get a little bit homesick sometimes," she adds. "I'm from Scotland, you see. You probably noticed the accent."

What a stupid thing to say! I take out a bag of boiled sweets and pop one in my mouth. Rhubarb and custard.

"My boyfriend and I made vodka with those the other week," Deborah says, interrupting the blissful moment when the flavours of the sweets infuse your mouth and remind you of more innocent times.

"That's nice," I say.

It's no good, I'm going to have to move away first. I take a few more shots of the llamas and walk on.

The sun plays havoc with my tired eyes and I'm just reaching for my sunglasses when I hear the girl's voice calling me, her running footsteps slapping the gravel path beyond the llamas enclosure.

"Excuse me! Stop!"

I turn round wondering what on earth can be the matter.

Deborah leans in close, making me shudder. She whispers in my ear, "Your skirt is caught up in your knickers," then with a giggle she sprints off back to the bench where one of the llamas is sitting playing the solo from *Will You* on her saxophone.

WHITE SAND COCOON

The tired sun is like a golden eye squinting beneath a heavy brow of cloud.

I watch him as he sits at the shabby dining table stabbing the keys of his laptop. How can he not be distracted by the setting sun and the mesmerizing view across the bay?

His face is screwed up and reminds me of my father's boxer dog. Every now and then he squeezes his lips between his thumb and forefinger. He is lost in the project. The project I know little about. He likes keeping me in the dark. He says it's better that way.

It know he's protecting me. He's like that; a beautiful soul. I never thought I could enter into a relationship with a man like Jacob.

"Come on, Louise, what do you really see in him? He has acne and scars, for goodness sake!"

Corinna just doesn't get it. Jacob calls her Little Miss Shallow or when he's in a grumpy mood, The Plastic One. Still, he never objects to our girly nights out when we're back on the mainland.

We chose this spot for its remoteness. I love the feel of warm, wet sand between my toes when we take our evening walks.

But there haven't been any evening walks for two days now, because of The Project. Jacob's big secret. The Project that always has a knock on effect on our lives.

"Work comes first," he's so fond of saying. "After you, of course!" and his face crumples like an old brown paper bag as he smiles; his eyes telling me all I need to know. I can never be in any doubt as to Jacob's feelings for me. No man has ever made me feel so at home in my own skin.

I look back at the view. The red-roofed boathouse on stilts; the tufted grass on the dunes blowing in the breeze like a bouffant hairdo. I never tire of looking out of this huge window. How can Jacob be so focused when it's all out there waiting for him?

"He's under a lot of pressure at work," I told Corinna on the phone last night. "I don't want to abandon him at a time like this. He feels safe when he knows he can cocoon himself against me in bed at night."

I can hear Corinna's disapproval leeching down the phone. She doesn't understand why I'm giving up the chance of a girly night in Brannigan's in exchange for a night of silence with a man who's under pressure. A man in fear of losing his job. A man who feels that financial security is the only thing keeping me here with him.

This afternoon I walked along the beach to Dunaverty Head. A man was sliding down the dunes with his two children. The sun made their golden hair look like miniature halos. Their laughter echoed all around me as I walked. Where was his wife? Was she sitting in a caravan in the holiday park behind them, doing a crossword or reading a book; making the most of the peace and quiet while her husband took them out to play?

I try to imagine Jacob and I with two golden-haired children. I've stopped nagging him about it lately. He may come round in his own time. The Project is one step closer to my dream. If he can pull it off, then that's a few more thousand pounds in the bank, which will shore us up for another precious year. How many more thousands of pounds and projects will it take to make him feel secure enough to take a chance?

This afternoon I photographed the old fishing vessel with the navy blue hull at anchor. I pictured our children scrambling over it, begging Jacob to take them out to sea.

I can picture his face creased up with anxiety and fear. No risks. Better to be safe than sorry.

And just when does he think the pressure will be off? When can he release the brakes and go hurtling down the hill towards an unknown fate? Just how much time does he need?

"Time is running out, Jacob," I tell him. "When are you going to stop chasing the project to end all projects? When does it stop?"

Once more my mind scrolls back to the man on the dunes with his children, hurtling down the slope to a soft, sandy landing. He knows they'll be safe. There are no pebbles on the beach; just warm, soft sand and a woman who is waiting for their return.

SKIN AND BONE

I sit at the table on the restaurant terrace, staring at the bleached out sky. Robin has gone inside to use the bathroom. It's been at least ten minutes since he spoke.

He'd ordered the dover sole again. I was vexed, because the reason we'd come to Hardy's was so that he could sample the traditional English food he'd eaten at boarding school. Liver, onions and bacon; beef stew and dumplings; cottage pie. Lots of red meat and potatoes. Just what he needed to feed him up.

I look down at our plates. The dribbles of sauce surrounding the fish skin and bones has congealed and the vegetables look listless and bored. The red wine gravy from my beef stew has dried in the sun. I wish the waiter would hurry up and take the plates away. I hate sitting in front of leftovers. The service has deteriorated since the last time we came.

"You were a long time," I say when he sits back down at the table. "More wine?"

He nods and shifts a little in his seat. I see the faintest

smear of vomit on his chin and my heart sinks. I really thought my youngest child was over this. I take my napkin and wipe it away.

I pour the chilled Chardonnay into our glasses and put the bottle back in the ice bucket. There's a third of a bottle left and I don't fancy staying around to drink it.

I reach across the table for Robin's hand. He seems distracted and it's not the sea view. The tinkling sound of the halyards are beginning to irritate me. It's a happy sound. A sound for different moments than this. I bitterly regret bringing Robin out for a meal. I thought the expense alone would make him eat everything on his plate.

"Robin, I'm sorry. We should have had lunch at home. I could have made you an omelet."

He seems to physically withdraw into himself. His cheeks are sunken in, his eyes seem lost in their sockets and his skin seems shrivelled like an old orange. He's old before his time.

"Don't worry, Mum," he says and pats my hand. "It makes a nice change to eat out."

BLESS HIM. He always did know how to make me feel better. Despite his illness, Robin provides comfort and support when I need it most. Like the time his dad left me for good. He struggled to break the bond between Robin and me. He admitted defeat in the end, just as all of Robin's girlfriends gave up the fight. There's a special something between a mother and son. Not everyone understands.

A burst of laughter from the next table brings me back to the present. Two men and two girls about the same age as Robin. They're strong, healthy and tanned. Robust twenty-somethings, probably students whose parents have slipped them a twenty pound note each to have a decent meal. Two empty wine bottles are up-ended in ice buckets on their table and the four of them are slinging back shots with their coffee. A pretty, freckled girl leans in to kiss her boyfriend on the lips. I look back at Robin who's staring at them with envy. How different things could have been for him.

"Shall we go, Mum?" he asks and signals the waiter for the bill.

I pour the rest of the wine into my glass and knock it back. I hate to see anything going to waste.

We walk along the beach afterwards and I'm thankful it's not the school holidays, otherwise it would be overrun with children. I look over at the ice-cream van. I'd love a '99. The perfect dessert on a sunny day.

"Fancy an ice-cream, Robin?"

A stupid question, I know. He just looks at me and gives me that wry smile of his.

We watch two gulls squabbling over some leftover chips. The sun aims its blinding glare at our faces and we turn away as one.

"Thanks for today, Mum. It shows you haven't given up hope for me."

I pull Robin towards me. "I'll never give up hope, Robin. I love you more than life itself."

I look over his shoulder and watch the gulls fly off towards the gently rolling waves. I feel Robin's thin frame against my ample one and squeeze him tighter.

7

GLAM ROCK AND SCRAMBLED EGGS

The first meal you ever cooked for me was scrambled egg on toast, not the spaghetti bolognese you'd promised the day before when we'd stood by the ancient radiator in the school crush hall where old boys names were carved onto wood plaques with gold lettering.

The eggs you made were a little sloppy, but I forgave you for that. After all, you were only fourteen. And remember how horrified you were that I put tomato ketchup on mine? And I felt sick, because you'd put too much butter on the toast. We didn't usually have butter in our house, as Mum was always on a diet, counting every calorie as if her life depended on it.

That was the day you got your first David Cassidy poster from *Jackie* magazine. You said you were going to put it up on the wall facing your bed, so that he was the last person you saw before falling asleep. You hoped you would dream about him and maybe you do. I hope so.

And remember that diary you kept? A page a day. It had a little brass lock and you kept the key for it around your neck. I felt so privileged when you allowed me to read some of it. You had dotted all the i's with a heart. There was a long description of Simon Hughes, I seem to remember. He was the lanky Sixth Former you fancied that year. I didn't see what you saw in him. He had spots and his legs were too skinny. Remember we used to watch him playing rugby from our classroom window?

You never did get to go out with him, did you? Such a pity. You had to make do with Mark Walters in the year above us. He took you to see *Love Story* and you had to lend him a tissue, because he couldn't hold back the tears. We waited and waited for a poster of Ryan O'Neil to appear in *Jackie,* but I don't think it ever did, unless we missed it.

The day of the scrambled eggs, we climbed up onto the roof of the lean-to, so we'd have a view of Simon Hughes' house. I almost broke my leg climbing back down the drain pipe and you wet yourself laughing.

And how annoyed we were when the new chart came out and we discovered *Amazing Grace* was Number One.

"Who are the Scots Dragoon Guards anyway?" you asked, "And what business have they got messing up the Top Forty like that? Only real musicians should be allowed to make a record!"

You were very opinionated in those days, Yvette.

We used to record the Top Forty on Sunday nights; our cassette players shoved right up in front of an old transistor. We'd cross our fingers, whispering, "Suzi, please let Suzi be Number One!" Or it might have been The Sweet or T-Rex, or whoever was our favourite that week. I remember lying in a bath drenched with Aqua Manda listening to the crackly sounds of '72.

And how Miss Wroxham told us off for wearing too much turquoise eyeshadow in her German class. Remember, we had to scrub it off in the girls' loos? I was most put out, because it was expensive. Mary Quant, no less.

I never imagined the scrambled egg lunch would be your last. That afternoon we scoured Chelsea Girl for bargains and I bought that vile brown corduroy bomber jacket. Remember? We thought it was the height of fashion and taste. Along with our denim flares and shirts with pointy collars. We bought one of those huge cream buns each from Hindley's and sat on a bench in the precinct to eat them, hoping Simon Hughes or the lad I fancied didn't walk past and see us with cream on our faces. Who was the lad I fancied? He had a nickname... Sam, that's right, but it wasn't his real name. I can't remember his real name. Funny, isn't it, how we forget these things when we get older?

I can't believe that it happened because of a row with your mum over using all the eggs. If you hadn't cooked scrambled eggs for me, then there'd have been some left for your mum to bake that special cake for her friend's birthday. She'd promised she'd take a coffee and walnut gateau into work the next day. But she didn't go to work the next day or the day after that.

You rowed about the eggs and you stormed off on your bike. I'll never forget that bike. It was dark green. A Ladies Raleigh Cycle, they said in *The Limeworth Herald* a few days later. There was a photograph of you in your school uniform with the caption: Have you seen this girl?

Andrew Stafford wasn't looking for someone to kill, the police said. You incited his anger somehow. All that anger that had been building up as he lay on a metal-framed bed in his quarters. He hated the army. Hated his Sergeant Major in particular. Sergeant Toft, the bully, who made his life a misery.

You bore the brunt of Andrew Stafford's anger, Yvette,

and I remember being gutted that you never got to hear *Metal Guru* by T-Rex or *School's Out* by Alice Cooper. The summer of 1972 was a roller-coaster, to use a modern day phrase. On the one hand I was incredibly sad at losing you, but on the other I was on cloud nine. That summer was brilliant, simply because I met David Elson. He took me for picnics in cornfields and chased me round the castle grounds. He also took me in his arms while I sobbed over you. He's now my husband, Yvette. We met up again last year after finding each other on one of those social networking sites. We were both divorced and looking for love. If we'd realised that love was staring us in the face in 1972, then we might have taken the plunge sooner. Still, youth is wasted on the young. Sorry, slip of the tongue again.

I come here every year, Yvette. I hope you enjoy me reminiscing. I will never forget you, because I haven't had a best friend like you since. Except perhaps my David.

I'm sorry it's only sweet peas today. Like me, they're a bit past their best, but their fragile petals remind me of you.

And we'll be having scrambled eggs on toast for tea tonight, just as we always do after I've visited you.

8

ALOPECIA AND A STRAY DOG

Day after day, alone on a hill. That's Marty. He dresses in rags and walks barefoot to tend his few remaining sheep. Tufts of their wool decorate the barbed wire boundaries of his land. Marty was a soldier once, but the locals have forgotten that. Now he's just The Fool On The Hill.

Marty ventures down to the village for supplies, side-stepping dozing fat caterpillars on the dusty farm track and trailing his calloused hands through the wild fuchsia bushes. All the way down the hill his gaze never wavers from the bright blue ocean view in front of him. Who knows what's on his mind? Is he thinking about his father who drowned trying to save a sinking vessel during a storm? Or of his mother who rowed out to sea and was never seen again? Or the baby brother whom they found with a pillow over his face?

Dora in the shop says Marty never speaks when he comes to buy his milk and bread. He simply nods a thank you when she gives him his change. Some say he's a rich man who has no idea what to do with his money. Others call him a murderer.

They say Marty hasn't left Muasdale for thirty years. Not since he went to fight a war no one believed in. They say he was hoping to be killed to atone for his sins. But I don't believe for one minute that Marty held that pillow over his sleeping brother's face.

"Alopecia," I tell the locals. "It's more common than you think."

Marty has been completely bald since he returned from The Falklands.

"It would have been the shock. Seeing his mates killed. Things like that, well, your body can't ignore it. The shock has to manifest itself somehow."

They look at me as if I'm as mad as Marty as I sip my pint and tell them stories of battle fatigue, shell-shock and post-traumatic stress disorder. It's my field, you see. I can see their eyes glaze over and suddenly the match on Sky is more appealing or there's a pressing game of darts to finish.

The day I was invited into Marty's house was the day the stray dog wouldn't leave. I watched him attempt to shoo it from his back door, which was practically rotting on its hinges. The dog simply cowered, then attempted to get back in.

"Bugger off, you mongrel!" I heard him shout. "Leave me alone, why can't you?"

I smiled. It was good to hear Marty hadn't lost his voice after all. Filled with a new confidence, I approached him, accompanied by the sound of bleating sheep and a whining dog.

"Marty? You don't know me. I'm Ben. I might be able to help you."

He frowned and shook his head. He watched as I crouched down and ruffled the dog's coat.

"Is he yours?" Marty asked. "If he is, take him and bugger off."

"I think he's a stray, Marty." I watched as the dog sidled up to his legs, looking up at him with imploring eyes. "He's taken a liking to you."

Reluctantly Marty allowed the dog to lick his hand, then chuckled. "He's probably hungry and thirsty, the poor old fella."

I followed man and dog into the house, which, to my surprise, was as neat as a new pin.

"Army training," Marty said. "Some things never leave you. Tea?"

It was the best cup of tea I'd ever tasted. Assam made in a bone china teapot and served in a matching cup and saucer.

"Only the best for visitors," Marty mumbled as he opened a packet of Nice biscuits.

Without further ado, the dog fed and watered, he began to tell me about The Battle Of Goose Green.

"Lost five of my best friends that day," he concluded and laid his hand on mine.

He didn't need to ask who I was. Sometimes you instinctively know who to trust and who to confide in.

I check on him most days. I've never set foot in his kitchen since. The dog died two days after he turned up at Marty's door. Death seemed to follow him around like a heavy sigh.

They still talk about The Fool On The Hill, but who is more deluded?

He sees the sun going down and the eyes in his head see the world spinning round.

9

COLOURS FADE TO BLACK AND WHITE

My life seems to be made up of spinning yo-yos. There they go in a kaleidoscope of colours like the stained glass in next door's window. Pinks, purples, yellow, reds and greens. This is my world.

We have steamed vegetables for tea. They arrived earlier today in a bio-degradable easily-to-fold-down box. All organic, of course and so fresh they hardly take any cooking. Mum doesn't buy supermarket vegetables. She says it's like eating plastic and goodness only knows how long they've been in transit.

We don't eat meat in this house. As far as Mum is concerned, I've never eaten meat, but I couldn't resist trying a bacon roll at Casey's house once and another time a tuna mayo sandwich. It was what everyone else was having and I didn't want to make a fuss or to be different from the others.

As I sit eating my corn-on-the-cob, melted butter dripping down my chin, I think about Delith Jones. She hadn't long joined our school before she was abducted. I liked her dark curly hair and goofy teeth. She was kind to me.

Now I can't step outside the front door without Mum or

Dad asking where I'm going and who with. They have a five step policy in place; things I have to do if I'm suspicious of anyone. The one I won't be able to do is to kick him in the wotsits. I mean, he'd just grab my leg, wouldn't he and then he'd see my knickers and he'd have won.

They still haven't found Delith, nor her body. At school we imagine what could have become of her. Anita says she thinks she's been strangled and dumped in the river. Casey says she's still alive and being kept in a locked-up shed at the bottom of someone's garden, and Paul Mallander says she's been battered to death with a brick.

I think a man and a lady who can't have babies and IVF hasn't worked for them have taken her to be their special little girl. Delith's probably wearing Mini Boden clothes and attending tap and ballet lessons in Primrose Hill like my cousin. A better life than this boring old town.

Mum says never to talk to strangers, but if I listened to her, then I'd never have made friends with Mr Timms at Number 53, nor his Polish lodgers who have very red faces and deep voices.

I'm sitting on the front garden wall waiting for Dad to come home and I'm playing with next door's tabby cat. Shilough, he's called. He spends more time at our house than next door. Mum says it's because they're rubbish pet owners and leave him locked outside most of the day. I pick long stalks of grass and flick them around to tease him. He seems to like that and plays for ages. When Mum's not looking I pour some full fat organic milk into an old bowl and give it to Shilough. She's told me hundreds of times not to encourage him, but he's so sweet, I can't resist and I'm sure next door don't feed him properly. Not Mr Timms at Number 53. The other side. The Whites.

Mr White is always in the corner shop buying firelighters. I had to ask Mum what they were. She said they were white blocks you put on an open fire to keep it from going out. I like the black box they come in. It has pretty orange flames on it. Mr White has whitish-grey hair and bright twinkly blue eyes. He never says hello and he shuffles. I've never seen him wearing shoes, only slippers; tartan ones with cream edging.

Mum says the Whites have a hoarding problem. I'm not really sure what that is, but their windows are dirty and they always have the curtains closed so you can't see inside. Mum says all sorts could be going on in there and no one would ever know.

For a moment I wonder whether Delith Jones is in there.

Mum says the Whites' property would be worth a fortune, if they did it up. They have a four-bedroom Victorian house like ours on the outskirts of town with all its original features. She says if it was renovated like ours, then it would be worth at least £600,000. I can't imagine that much money. Lots of weekly shops, and super deluxe veg boxes from Wild and Free Organics, anyway.

"Don't go wandering off!" Mum shouts from the front door. "Bath time in ten minutes!"

That means at least twenty. She'll either be texting Auntie Carole or having a sneaky glass of wine before Dad gets home. Or both.

Shilough lies down so that I can tickle his belly. I do it with a stalk of grass, because my hands go all blotchy and red if I touch his fur. I get that from Dad. It's why we can't have a cat of our own, he says.

I hear the Whites' front door slam and look up.

Mrs White levers herself down the front steps. Mum says she's a martyr to her arthritis. She has a brown and red checked shopping bag over her arm. She never speaks and always looks at the floor. Her hair is dyed a weird orangey colour, as if she's left the dye on too long or something. She ignores Shilough, and he doesn't seem bothered.

When she turns the corner, I dare myself to run to their front door and lift the letterbox. It's something I've been trying to do for ages. I just want to peer into their hallway to see the newspapers and old milk cartons; to see if what Mum says is true. It's so dark in there, though, I can't see a thing. I fiddle around in my pocket till I find what I need.

My heart is thrumming like the old traction engines Dad took me to see at the steam fair last week. I look left and right, then just as I'm lifting the letterbox, I see a shadow pass by the window and I shiver. Someone is watching me. My mouth goes dry and it tastes like I've been munching on metal. For a moment I'm frozen; as if my feet are cemented into the floor. I feel as if I'm going to wet myself, then I hear Shilough's miaow, which makes everything seem normal and safe. I turn from the door and run back to our garden. I should go inside now, but I want to see what happens.

Dad will be home from work any minute now. I start looking for his bike. He always cycles to work. The only time we use the car is for holidays and weekend trips to visit family. Anita's mum calls us 'eco-warriors' whatever they are. Dad says we're Green.

It's then I hear a tap-tapping on the window. I turn around expecting to see Mum calling me in. Tap tap-tap. I can't see Mum's face at the window. Then I look next door.

The Whites' curtain is twitching and I see a fist at the window. Tap tap-tap.

I stay on our side of the path and walk a little closer to the window. I can see a smudgy shape through the thin curtain. It's probably creepy Mr White. I remember Mum and Dad's five step policy regarding strangers. The first step is to run into our house as fast I can, if I'm near home, that is.

My legs won't move.

The fist isn't big enough for Mr White's. It's a child's fist knocking the window, I'm sure.

"Molly! Inside now!" Mum shouts.

I should do as I'm told, but I need to know if it really is Delith Jones knocking at the window. Perhaps the Whites have half-buried her beneath piles of old newspapers and plastic milk cartons?

I creep closer; as close as I dare. I can see an orangey glow through the curtains, then smoke. Someone is coughing; choking even.

Mr White and his firelighters. A box every day. Why does he need so many? What if he's bought them to help set his house on fire and burn the evidence?

I hear a bicycle bell behind me and Dad's waving and grinning like a loony. Suddenly everything seems less scary.

"What are you doing spying on the Whites, Molly, love?"

I put my fingers to my lips and call him over. I can smell the smoke now and the orange glow is brighter. I feel excited and wonder whether I'll see that kaleidoscope of colours I see when Dad has a bonfire in the back garden. I'm just about to ask him, but he's busy talking into his Iphone.

I NEVER DID GET to have a bath that night. Mum said it was far too late by the time the fire brigade had gone.

Delith's parents bought me a big cuddly cat and a box of chocolates. I can't understand why, because I didn't do anything.

Mr and Mrs White don't live next door anymore.

Mum says they're in custody, whatever that means. Perhaps they live in a world that's yellow and thick.

The RSPCA man was nice, but he said I couldn't keep Shilough. Maybe Dad told him about my rash.

I accidentally told Casey's mum and dad about the matches when they were feeding me more bacon sandwiches one Saturday morning. I only fed two through the letter box so that I could see inside a bit better.

They promised not to tell.

There isn't a kaleidoscope of colours next door now. The door is charred black against the white walls and now the Whites have gone, so have my spinning yo-yos and my world is a dull shade of grey.

10

HELENA

Helena is melting dark chocolate in a copper pan. The hem of her moth-eaten dress, once black, now faded to gun-metal grey, is haphazardly curtseying to the dirty floor. She gazes with longing at the smooth, shiny surface of the chocolate, deciding to throw in a handful of gritty currants she has found at the back of a forgotten cupboard.

The kitchen is full of cupboards, most of which Helen has never opened. Their black secrets are closed to her. Helena is untroubled by unfamiliar corners of her house. She enjoys obscurity and otherness.

She dips a leathery forefinger into the pan and tastes the harsh sweetness which cloys in the back of her throat. She smiles and remembers the salty oyster-like substance she'd swallowed just hours before.

Her mouth is full again; tasting him, surrounding him, willing herself not to choke.

Helena sees his wild-dog face, his bared teeth and bristly chin seeking out her marshmallow thighs. A savage cat-like tongues probes her depths. Helena shudders, then pours the dark-studded liquid into a mould and waits.

APPLE BLOSSOM FLUTTERS across the pavement in the May-time breeze and Helena quickens her pace to escape the fresh white pictures which come unbeckoned into her head. It's no use. Shy brides bow beneath a shower of confetti and dainty bridesmaids skip about, pointing their satin-toed slippers in time to peals of laughter.

Helena winces and begins to run. The house is within reach. Its grimy windows leer at her. She smiles and pushes open the heavy wooden door, brushing aside old withered creeper and foraging brambles.

Helena retreats into a back room and tugs at the heavy velvet drapes to block out the intrusive May sun.

EVERY DAY HELENA completes the same ritual. She searches the streets, but can no longer find the merest trace of his sour breath and matted hair.

She listens for his deep-throated whistle or his brittle laugh, but no sound reaches her jet-studded ears.

She longs to feel the sweet stickiness between her thighs to prove that she is alive.

Where is he?

EVERY NIGHT HELENA lights candles whose rich scent once lured him inside. Burnt out joss sticks litter the hearth. The music is always the same. Deep, resonant, funereal. He can be reached, she just needs to remember the right combination. The pattern must be complete.

Chocolate, its bitter-sweet smell colliding with musky Eastern scents and the music.

What else?

Red wine, ash-trays spilling their contents onto faded gold sofas and crumbs littering the threadbare carpet.

Helena scatters torn satin cushions over the floor, lies back, pulling strands of thick dark hair over her ample breasts and she waits.

A dog barks out in the street. Someone is kicking a can and a woman's laughter, rich and throaty, cuts through the empty night air.

A door creaks open, and he is there.

HELENA LIFTS his hand to her cheek and licks the salty surface. She wonders how those harsh, grainy hands could have handled such delicate confections to display in her father's shop window.

His words are like worms, slithering and squirming in Helena's head. She raises her arms and clasps her silver-ringed hands over her ears. That's it; she can spew them out now, biting their fat bodies in two and letting them wriggle to the floor.

Broken words.

Helena urges him on and on. This time it is different. His mad-dog face is expressionless and mute. Without words he is powerless. His tongue remains locked inside his head.

She gazes into his clear, blue eyes; then steps into their

unfathomable depths... and beyond... striving to piece together the broken fragments of his mind.

It is hopeless.

The fragments have become shards of glass, razor sharp and untouchable. Blood begins to seep out into the filthy carpet. Helena gasps and starts to shake his skinny frame until he rolls over and away from her. He can never desert her again.

IT IS LATE AUTUMN. Helena walks slowly. One...two. She must get it right; for this is her wedding march. One...two. One...two. She hears the music in her head, and clasps the posy of cornflowers closer to her silk clad bodice. One...two.

The train of her wedding dress is leaving a trail of sand. The shoreline is the altar, but it continues to recede. He is not there. Helena gasps and clutches her posy tighter still, urging herself on. One...two. One...two. No, she's walking too quickly. She should have waited. Brides are always late, aren't they? And bridegrooms?

Helena reaches the shore and bends down to pick up a coral pink shell. Its interior has been washed clean by the waves and she strokes it with a ringless finger, then casts it into the foam. An angry sea. Clear blue, like his eyes. Or cornflower blue?

Helena tosses her posy to the wind and shakes the wispy veil from her head. Her black hair struggles out of the carefully placed pins and whips away the tears from her thread-veined cheeks.

Helena picks up the dead slug shape from the grubby pink cushion and places it on a bone china plate with cornflower blue edges; an engagement present from a crochety old aunt who is now dead.

There is a furious buzzing in Helena's gloomy kitchen, as a crazed bluebottle finally lands on a length of grubby white satin, which hangs from the airer. Helena turns to watch it stumble over a loose pearl button and smiles.

She wrenches the dress from its hanger and tugs it over her head. More pearls escape the worn stitching.

Helena takes the dirty copper pan from the kitchen table and begins to snap off large pieces of chocolate, hurling them onto the caked-on surface. She pulls the shiny fabric further over her lumpy thighs, grasping the singed wooden spoon tighter as she stirs the melting chocolate.

It's a nice day for a white wedding.... There is music in her head once more.

A viscous lump of dark mixture splashes onto her breasts. Helena looks down, swipes it away with a plump finger and, on seeing the stained fabric, begins to sob.

11

SURFER BOY

I watch the boys dive off the pier with their surf boards tucked under their arms. So young and so foolish. One surfaces and swims out to where the other surfers are making the most of the crashing breakers. I still can't see the other boy. People are leaning over the pier as far as they dare, panic swarming over their faces.

I know he's dead. He'll have hit his head on one of the cast iron pier struts, unable to fight the pressure of the deep water, slowing sinking towards the sea bed. He'll pop up later, his head wound scavenged by hungry sea creatures. I walk away, unable to bear looking at the hope and terror in people's faces.

I walk back towards the amusement arcades and the donkeys tied up to the railings. A tang of salty air hits me and I realise how hungry I am. It's when I'm sitting in The Sea View Restaurant tucking into my fish and chips that I hear the sirens. I glance out of the window and see the tourists frozen like ice sculptures as it slowly dawns on them that something major has happened and someone might be dead.

You probably think I'm callous. Hard. Blame my job, if you have to. I see this sort of thing all the time. I'm the one who's constantly under pressure to get the results expected of me. I'm the one who has to make copious notes and see that the poor, pathetic things are dispatched in the correct manner. The only time I've ever been reprimanded was when I had dandruff on the shoulder of my morning coat. One of the mourners complained. Can you believe that? You'd think they'd have more important things to worry about. Like mourning their dead relative, perhaps?

I tip the waitress slightly more than usual. It'll be a good month, this. I can tell. We've already had six more funerals than usual for September.

I climb the steep step, which lead away from the beach. I could have taken the cliff railway, but it's daylight robbery. A tourist attraction and no more. They sit in those wooden cabins with the stained glass windows and imagine they live in the Victorian age. The women probably have romantic visions of wearing crinolines and carrying a parasol. The men, of wearing frock coats and top hats. Of course, the latter is what I wear every day to work. A smart gentleman who could easily slot in to the 1880s, that's me.

I don't like the modern day hearses. The best occasions are those when they hire the six horses with black feathers between their ears and the stately black carriage edged with gold.

I was born too late. This modern era isn't for me.

By the time I reach the town square, I hear mutterings amongst the shopkeepers closing for business. Mobile phones make news travel faster. Texts must have been flying from the pier to the town about the boy who was foolish enough to jump off the pier. He's a local lad. Not some tourist who'll be buried back at home. I almost feel like rubbing my hands together.

I do feel for his parents, I do. Who will break the news to them? Do they live in one of the streets named after gemstones or in the big houses that frown down upon the beach like stern uncles?

I look at my watch. What a way to spend my day off. I should have gone into Redcar or Middlesborough and put a bet on. I could have scoured the charity shops for a present for my old Ma or bought a new jumper from Marks and Sparks.

But no. What have I done? Trundled around my hunting ground looking for business. I get a gut feeling about these things. I knew there'd be a customer today.

As soon as I walk into the flat and my eyes glance upon the pewter scythe my friend bought me as a joke, I know something is wrong.

"Ma? Are you there?"

I walk into the living room and see the back of her head. Phew! She's watching a re-run of *Escape To The Country*. All is well.

"Cup of tea and a slice of cake, Ma?"

She doesn't answer. I go and get it anyway. Her Saturday teatime treat. It's only when I take it in to her that I see her head is lolling to one side. I take her pulse.

I can't even guess how long I sit there, watching and willing it not to be true.

I look out of the window and see the pinpricks of light signalling the end of the day. The sun slips down in the blink of an eye.

Never did I think I'd be able to identify with that surfer boys' parents... until now.

Two customers in one day. He'll be so pleased with me, my boss. He's been putting a lot of pressure on me lately. Business was slack in the spring.

But he's not having this one. She's mine.

TWISTED SHEETS

The room smells of sex. They'd scrabbled between the stained sheets like sea urchins or conk-eyed crabs. Rumpled and twisted swathes of Egyptian cotton; the room sucking in her jealousy like oysters through a straw. She'd scratched his back and teethmarks branded his shoulders. Rolling over. He was hers and no one else's, she'd said, his semen spilling from her mouth like opals. The pillow is still propped up as she left it. Cold coffee and her creased-spine paperback on the bedside table. He clears them away then smoothes out the rapidly cooling sheet, ready for her replacement.

CAMELS IN A FIELD

The day she saw camels in a farmer's field was the day things changed for Ellen.

She was driving round the roundabout minding her own business and there they were, munching grass, humps proudly silhouetted against a bleached out sky. Desert creatures in a lush green field.

When Ellen saw the Big Top at the next roundabout, she breathed a sigh of relief. Thank goodness. Her brain wasn't addled. She wasn't hallucinating. Perhaps she'd have a glass of wine with lunch, after all.

She was meeting her old friend, Milly, at The Longshoot. They taught together from 1990-1992 in a sprawling comprehensive with a bad reputation.

"It's a science and technology college now, you know," Milly told her over deep fried Camembert in breadcrumbs.

Ellen slathered on cranberry jelly and pretended to look interested.

"We were lucky to get out when we did, Ellen. I think we landed on our feet, don't you?"

Milly got a job as Head of Department in a grammar school and was quickly promoted to Deputy Head.

"You meeting Dominic just after you moved to that private school was a stroke of luck, don't you think?"

Most people saw Dominic as a stroke of luck.

"I mean, that top you're wearing must be designer and that bag, Ellen, is to die for."

Elle smiled and laid down her knife and fork. To die for. Quite. Twenty years with Dominic and she wanted to die. She'd been slowly killing herself for years.

"And your car! I wish I could afford a BMW convertible on my salary! How is Dominic's business what with the recession and everything?"

Ellen suppressed a yawn and signalled to the water for another glass of wine. She should have ordered a bottle when they first arrived. It would have been cheaper.

"Business is buoyant. One of the few in the country that is, I imagine. Still, Dominic has all those overseas investments, which helps. We're thinking of moving to Dubai. Did I mention that on the phone? Anyway, have you met anyone yet? Still doing the internet dating?"

Ellen couldn't resist. Now it was her turn to make Milly feel uncomfortable.

Milly shrugged. "It's okay. I still haven't met Mr Right. I do go out on some nice dates, though. It has become rather a hobby. Most are divorcees looking for a woman with property and money. They want to be able to slip their feet under the table and not worry about where the money's coming from to pay the bills."

Ellen took a long swig of chilled Chardonnay and thought how liberating it would feel to have one's pick of men. To be taken out on dates several times a week with no real expectations. No demands on her body. No arguments.

No moods, no sulks, no nagging. To be able to spend one's money as one chose.

The waiter took their starter plates away and came back with platters of mixed grill and a large sirloin steak with mushrooms and onion rings. He placed a bowl of chips in the middle of the table to share, which Milly immediately began to pick at with long fingers and well manicured finger nails.

Ellen felt like a horse fly on gorse. She'd suddenly lost her appetite.

All her friends seemed to be ganging up on her these days. If they weren't going on about her weight, then they'd mention her wayward twenty-year-old daughter or the fact that Ellen drank too much. As if she needed telling. Then there were the pills. The ones she sneaked into her mouth with sips of water when she thought no one was looking. She really shouldn't be driving. Perhaps she should order a taxi, then Dominic or the gardener could pick the car up later.

"Milly, tell me. Where do you see yourself in ten years time?" Ellen asked, fiddling with a mushroom.

"Retired. Travelling the world. Tending my garden. All the things a retired single woman of my means tend to do. And you?"

"Dead as a fucking dodo, Milly, that's where I see myself. Six foot under in an anonymous graveyard somewhere."

Milly's cutlery clattered against her plate. "Ellen! Don't say such things!"

"Why not, Milly? Is death such a taboo subject? Look, my father died at fifty; my mother died at sixty and both sets of grandparents were dead by the time they were sixty-five. The odds are stacked against me. So," and Ellen chinked her glass against her friend's, "let's live for today, I say."

Milly stood up, her face mottled and puce. "I'm going to the Ladies. I think you should stick to the water and order a dessert."

THE CAMELS WERE STILL in the field when Ellen drove home. They were lying down dozing in the watery sunlight of late afternoon.

Perhaps Dubai was the answer? She'd watched a programme about an ex-air stewardess who'd received a shocking pink E-Type Jaguar from an Arab prince in 1970. There were photos of her posing on the bonnet. Ellen knew then that she'd been born too late. She, too, could have worn a smart uniform, joined the mile-high club and been given presents by rich oil tycoons from the Middle East.

Dominic's Lexus was on the drive when she got home. She'd tell him about Dubai, about the pen-pal from Abu Dhabi she'd been keeping a secret and the jewellery she'd pawned once she'd left the pub. She wouldn't mention Milly and the wasted food. Being left with the bill when Milly didn't return from the toilet.

Ellen opened the front door and the smell hit her. Something was rotting in the kitchen. Prawns? Eggs?

"Darling, I'm home!"

Ellen imagined the camels raising their heads on hearing her voice. Batting their long soft eyelashes at her, before spitting in her face.

She stepped over Dominic on the way to the fridge. Her appetite had returned.

14

RED MEAT

Vera pokes her finger into a pool of congealing gravy. White globs of fat have settled on the top. Nick complained earlier when she said about cooking roast lamb. Said it wasn't good for you. Reminded her what the doctor said about his heart and his blood pressure. He should have been back from the pub over an hour ago.

Vera pours another glass of wine and looks out of the window at the storm. Raindrops tap dance on the patio and Stubby Hall is obliterated from view by a white-out. The noise is almost unbearable. Nick still hasn't sorted the blocked guttering and now water sluices down onto the flat roof of the porch like Niagara Falls.

Nick hasn't taken a coat.

She's eaten her own supper, mopped up the fatty gravy with a slice of claggy white bread and put the plate in the dishwasher. She wonders whether to cut herself a slice of cheesecake or whether she'd better wait so that they can eat dessert together.

The storm abates and night sneaks in almost without

her noticing. Her Sunday night drama plays out to an accompaniment of dripping water from the guttering. The porch ceiling looks as if it's about to cave in. Another job for Nick to attend to when he returns.

She's just about to slide the dried up mess of his roast dinner into the pedal bin, when she hears his key in the door.

Nick is wearing different clothes and a tipsy smile.

"Just going to pack, then I'll be out of your hair," he tells her.

"Your supper, Nick. Roast lamb."

"What did I tell you about red meat, Vera?" he shouts from the bedroom.

Vera waits. When he reappears, he drops a cheque into her lap.

"Rent. Back-dated."

Once he's gone, she indulges in tears and the rest of the Chardonnay. Her sister's right. Vera is too needy. And now she needs to look for another lodger.

15

NO OIL FOR HOGMANAY

T he sea is the colour of pewter. We stroll along the beach hand-in-hand. Our usual Boxing Day walk. It's gusty today and I'm glad I've worn my thickest coat. Tony is shivering. He's wearing a T-shirt under his black leather jacket. The Ramones T-shirt I bought him for Christmas.

We're heading towards The Hope and Anchor. I am, anyway. I'm already anticipating a large gin and tonic and can picture the ice and lemon floating amongst the bubbles.

"I think I'll have the chicken pie again," says Tony. "Always the best option at The Hope, don't you agree?"

Tony will drink a pint of orange juice and eat every last morsel on his plate.

Children, animals, family. That's what Christmas always represented to me. But this year, we haven't had any of that. We are childless. Tony's parents live in Bahrain. We don't have pets. It's just the two of us.

And what did we do? Sat in front of the TV most of the day. A roaring log fire and a sad little artificial Christmas tree the only evidence of Christmas. I couldn't even be both-

ered to cook a turkey dinner. We had a coq au vin cooked in
the slow cooker and served with jacket potatoes. Tony didn't
seem to mind.

Christmas Day was fuelled by sherry, a perfectly chilled
bottle of Chablis, a nice full-bodied Shiraz, brandy and port
with coffee and mints. Maybe a Hendrick's gin in there
somewhere. Oh, and the pink champagne at breakfast. How
could I have forgotten? Tony had just the one glass.

"Did your mother phone earlier?" Tony asks me now, as
we walk past the redundant beach tractors, kicking at trails
of seaweed.

I shake my head. "This is the second year running now,"
I say, almost to myself.

Tony is watching my face. Looking for signs that I'm
going to crumble; ready to hold out his arms to me.

My parents disowned me some time ago. I don't blame
them. They'd had enough. Fed-up of me reeling in at 4am.
Vomiting over the bathroom floor; sometimes not even
making it that far. Mother guarding me as I slept, in case I
choked on my own vomit. Washing soiled sheets where I'd
lost control of my bladder or my bowels. Critically ill. Physically and mentally fucked.

Tony squeezes my hand. "Don't think about it.
Not today."

He pushes open the door to the pub and the warmth
enfolds us like a parent. Jovial voices wash up from the
public bar.

"And we haven't any oil for Hogmanay. Can you believe
it? Bastards won't deliver till after the New Year."

We find a table near the window and pick up the menus.
We both know we'll choose the pie and chips. We always do,
but there's always that anticipation that something new will
magically appear.

"Drink?" asks Tony.

I think about the gin and tonic. Maybe a schooner of sherry? What is the tradition on Boxing Day? A stiff whisky downed in the cold accompanied by misty breath while waiting to ride to hounds?

"I'll just have a coffee," I say, smiling up into his olive-skinned face.

I watch him walk to the bar, admiring his pert bum in tight blue jeans. I'm a lucky girl.

I look out of the window at Huntcliff Nab standing proud above the waves, cradling this whole coastline; hugging it to her bosom like a loving mother. This will do for now.

16

LADY ELEANOR

A woman is never more beautiful than when she's unaware of being watched.

Eleanor is in her bathing costume; pale with freckled skin, the sun picking out the golden highlights in her hair. She's helping Jack make a sandcastle. I'm sitting on a rock, book in hand, but I can't concentrate. Eleanor takes all of my attention. I want to go over and lick the salt of the sea from her skin. I want to feel those delicate orbs of breast in my hands and to cup her Mound of Venus in my hand. Holidays and sunshine are about sex and the sea. We revert to our primeval state. But now it's Jack's time. Eleanor is brilliant with him, and no one would ever know he wasn't her own son.

"You look gorgeous when your make-up has been sweated away by the heat of the sun and your lipstick eaten off with kisses and ice cream," I tell her later.

She smiles and my heart flips.

Jack is getting fractious. He's tired and needs a nap. We walk slowly back to the hotel, Jack holding Eleanor's hand and chatting about the beach. I love listening to the two of them. Their words are like droplets of liquid gold, dripping onto my heart.

"Don't dress up. Don't re-do your make-up. Let's go out just as you are with dried sweat between your breasts and smudgy black lines around your eyes," I tell Eleanor when we get back to the room.

We're using the excellent babysitting service the hotel offers. Jack has been bathed and fed with a child's box of mini fish and chips on the way home.

"Don't be silly, Ray. I can't go out like this!"

"Of course you can. Go on, I dare you! It'll turn me on and I'll give you the night of your life," I tell her and pull her onto the bed. Jack is absorbed in a DVD, so Eleanor and I play around a little.

"I'd planned to wear my new maxi dress tonight. You can't deny me the pleasure of that, Ray. And I love applying my make-up. It chills me out. A bit of pampering. You can't beat it. I guess you have to be female to understand that," she teases and tickles me under my chin. She nibbles my ear lobe, then gets up from the bed.

Eleanor is one of the most wonderful women I've ever met. And there have been a lot of women in my time.

Jack is asleep and we creep out like thieves.

We sit outside an old-fashioned pub on wooden picnic benches. I'm suffering from false memory, as I was certain this pub overlooked the beach, but I'm wrong. There's a busy road in front of it and the dirty river flows half-heartedly on the other side. I wanted this to be a romantic drink before dinner. I hope Eleanor isn't disappointed. I look at her. She's smiling at a man on the table opposite and it's like a knife to my chest.

The same types are drinking here as before. Bikers and ruddy-faced Cornish men. 'Before' being the time I visited this place with Fran, Jack's mum. It was a sunny evening just like now. I can picture Fran and me sitting at that table over there, the one to the right of the front door, the locals making us feel like one of the crowd. It's different now and I feel agitated. It's not right. It's not how I wanted it to be. I was drinking real ale back then and Fran, a pint of cider. I remember how quickly her cheeks turned red. Instead, I'm drinking gin and tonic, and Eleanor is sipping a glass of chilled Chardonnay. She has put on make-up and showered away the sea-salty-sweat from her body. She smells of body lotion and that sweet perfume she wears. It doesn't feel right. It's not earthy enough. Fran was earthy. Fran was solid and real.

And where is that funny little café where we had tea and scones? It had stuffed animals behind glass, fixed in frames on the walls. We had some kind of disagreement about what to eat, as I recall. Fran was so fussy about her food.

Eleanor's looking as serene as ever, but confused.

"When are we going to eat, Ray? This wine has gone straight to my head."

I smile. Where are we going to eat?

Where did Fran and I eat dinner that time? I can't remember. Isn't it funny how our memory condenses everything as if to make more room? Memory becomes like a compressed file ready to download onto the MP3 player of our mind.

New beginnings. I shudder a little in the cool of the evening and finish my drink. I've hardly spoken a word to Eleanor. She's away with the fairies, watching the blue lights over by the harbour. I catch her laughing at something the biker guy opposite her has said. Does she fancy him? He's giving her the once-over and I want to punch him. No, Ray. Be calm. It's all fine. Just finish the drinks and put your arm around her and escort her to a nice restaurant for dinner. This is a fresh start. Don't fuck it up.

My memory is returning like a long-lost friend. The restaurant has a name with a Z in it. Rizanni's? Zaldo's? Something Italian.

We walk towards the town centre. Eleanor seems distant, and I wonder if she's thinking about the biker guy.

"Okay?" I ask. This isn't going well. I'm too preoccupied with the past. The feeling of not belonging is becoming more acute as the day goes on. Eleanor and Jack are very much an item. Together. A pair. But we're not a team. Not yet.

"Do you think you're good enough for her?" my brother asked a week ago. "She's not your usual type."

I wanted to strangle him with my bare hands.

And as our feet rap the Cornish pavements, I feel the beat of a breaking heart.

It isn't working. She's too good for me.

"Eleanor?" I stop and we stand under a streetlight. "Are you happy?"

I study her face. She's thinking about it. And she's smiling. Eleanor always smiles.

"I was just about to ask you the same thing, Ray. You seem preoccupied. Is there something bothering you?"

How can I answer? There's always something bothering me.

Fran.

"No, I'm fine. You look beautiful."

We walk to the restaurant. Zizzi's. Italian. Breadsticks, olive oil, pasta and an overwhelming taste of tomato. The Chianti and the Amaretto save the day.

Back at the hotel, Jack is sleeping the sleep of the innocent. Something I haven't been able to do for a long time.

Eleanor is in the en-suite bathroom, brushing her teeth, moisturising and all those finicky things women do before bed. I tap my foot on the floor. Fidget. Drum my fingers on the bedside table. Take a bottle of brandy from the mini bar. Walk to the window and look out at the mist and listen to the shushing of the waves breaking on the shore.

I sense Eleanor behind me. She leans into me and I feel her dainty breath on the back of my neck.

"Bed?" she asks, softly.

"Brandy?" I ask. "Fetch a glass. It's good."

We drink in silence, sitting on the balcony, the breeze tickling our faces. Eleanor goes to fetch her bathrobe.

She sits back down, and I admire her bare feet. Pale. Prominent veins, one shaped like a devil's trident and red painted toe-nails. My thoughts lurch back to Fran. So much blood.

Too much blood.

"Penny for them?" says Eleanor stretching out her legs and staring up at the stars.

"They're worth far more, babe," I tell her and knock back the last of the brandy. "Bed?"

I lead her to the four poster and we slowly make love. Easing into each other. Competent, warm and tender. Her sighs mingle with the sounds of the ocean.

Jack turns over in his sleep and murmurs, 'Mummy'.

Eleanor smiles; that beautiful smile that infuses me with light and life.

I start to hum the song. *Lady Eleanor*.

And Fran doesn't intrude on my thoughts till I dream the dream. That dream. The dream infused with blood drenched organs. What is it like to drown in your own blood, Fran?

"She's vomiting blood," I cried to the hospital staff, who had a special name for it that I've long since forgotten.

"Dad?"

Jack wakes at dawn, and I pad over to his bed and take him in my arms.

Lady Eleanor sleeps on, oblivious.

17

GETTING IT OFF HER CHEST

Myrah sits down next to the golden rods, listens to the bees for a few moments, then looks down and shrugs her left breast out of the white lacy bra and weighs it in her hand. It is satisfyingly heavy, yet not ponderously so. After the mastectomy she'll ask them if she can keep it as a souvenir.

Adrian is taking it worse than she is. He's gone silent, hugging his grief inside himself, putting on a brave smile whenever he catches her looking at him. He's already mourning the breast, no doubt remembering touching it, stroking it, rolling his tongue around the delicate pink nipple or nibbling it mischievously.

His premature mourning incenses her. What about her? What about the MA in Literature she never got round to doing? No time to put things right. Her oncologist has given her leaflets, she's read case studies in books from the library, but nothing can assuage her terror.

Almost every night she dreams about the girl sitting in the road. A thin plait is draped over her left shoulder like an asp. Myrah wakes up sweating and trembling with something akin to desire. Adrian always assumes she's having nightmares about the breast. Myra wonders if Adrian imagines her dream as a huge growth with roots dangling down, growing larger and larger until it fills their whole lives.

The sun slides behind a cloud and Myrah looks up. The greyness is tinged with gold. A hint of a gift. Perhaps she has two healthy breasts, after all? Perhaps she's going to live for at least another thirty years?

Myrah now cups both breasts in her hands. She's sure they feel heavier and more tender than usual. Her stomach, usually concave, is now gently rounded. Myrah lifts her cotton skirt and moves her right hand to her abdomen. The breasts and abdomen, fecund, essentially female.

"I'm a leg man myself," Adrian told her once when they were in bed. She'd felt insulted. He'd laughed and pushed her thighs apart, nuzzling their softness.

Myrah decides to go into the house to lie down. The doctors have told her to get plenty of rest. Her bedroom is a cool place. The muslin drapes allow just enough light in to give the afternoon promise, yet shade her eyes from the glare. The lightness of the pine furniture, the soft cream lightshades and rugs make her feel tranquil as soon as she enters the room.

She lies on top of the white cotton duvet, fragilely embroidered with tiny yellow flowers.

A shimmer of a breeze creeps in and caresses her body, now naked.

Myrah smoothes her hands down over her breasts with a sigh. Soon she will only be able to feel pleasure on her right side; she sees her body after the operation as two separate sections. One for pleasure, the other remote, as if it doesn't belong to her anymore. It has betrayed her.

She drifts into daydreams, accompanied by the high-pitched scream of a hedge cutter.

She sees the girl again. This time she is lying in the road, naked and in pain. Myrah longs to pick her up. She wants to hold the child tightly to her, but the girl is merely a picture, an image of so many innocent victims of war. Myrah doesn't feel real. Myrah wishes she'd spent more time getting to know herself. She feels like a shadow drifting around her home, gliding over the spaces her body used to fill with exuberance and vitality. She remembers the parties they had every summer, when she got drunk and danced from room to room.

"Am I dead?" she asks Adrian later that evening.

He frowns, sighs and ignores her.

Adrian can't bear to breathe the same air as those people who court illness and death. He wants the rest of humanity to run with him and finish the race.

That night Myrah's kissing a woman; someone she knows, but not quite. The passion she feels is quite exceptional. She can't remember at what point she realises it's Adrian she's kissing instead. Once she's aware it's her husband making love to her, her passion withers and shrinks back to wherever it came from. They continue to make love, but Myrah is drifting in and out of sleep – her body on auto pilot.

She's the important one now. Adrian filters into the house after work, drinks whisky, eats supper, then goes to his study to write reports. After the operation she knows it will only be a matter of time before he vanishes completely.

THE NEXT MORNING everything is yellow. The sun is bursting

through the thin curtains, penetrating Myrah's thoughts. She is showered with seeds spurting from the centre of a giant sunflower. The seeds are entering her every orifice, impregnating her with vitality and life.

When she wakes Adrian has gone. Left early for work to ensure he remains the conscientious one in the company. Myrah's sure he's considered an arse-licker by his colleagues. She imagines him at the office, smug and in control.

Myrah stands at the kitchen window imagining the cancer spreading to her other breast, her throat, her liver. She feels faint, grabs the back of a kitchen chair, then sits down at the table. She takes her orange notebook and writes down the items she'll order from the Rigby and Peller catalogue, which arrived in the morning post.

She's been buying expensive lingerie for weeks now, putting lacy bras, satin bras and pure silk bras on her credit card, wearing them under see-through tops for the sheer hell of it. Myrah feels it's important to make the most of her assets while she still has two of them.

She stockpiles food from the best supermarkets and delicatessens, so she can completely indulge herself on these decadent days. Sometimes she ventures out to expensive restaurants and experiences a thrill when she places her credit card on top of the bill, knowing she won't be alive to pay it.

Today, she takes fresh eggs from her doorstep delivered by the local milkman. The yolks are orange, just as they should be. Myrah breaks the eggs into a pan, pours in thick Jersey milk, a spoonful of double cream, and stirs carefully. She then adds slivers of smoked salmon and freshly ground black pepper.

Myrah serves her meals on Wedgewood bone china, part

of a set given to them on their wedding day. It doesn't matter anymore if the plates get broken or chipped. She thinks she might as well make the most of it while she can.

She takes her meal up to the bedroom and slips off her kimono. Myrah sprawls naked on the bed, the duvet between her thighs, and eats hungrily, spilling fragments of egg and salmon on the pillow she is using as a tray. She slides open her bedside table drawer and takes out the anthology of lesbian short stories. She's been hiding them from Adrian, because she knows it will make him feel more insecure than he is all ready. Her free hand reaches for the delicate folds of flesh nestling amongst an abundance of black pubic hair. Myrah's short gasping cries bounce off the oyster coloured walls as she reaches orgasm. The Wedgewood plate tumbles from her pillow and smashes on the wooden floor.

Myrah giggles at the irony of it and goes to take a bath. She picks up a copy of *Northanger Abbey* from the bookcase on the landing.

She's re-reading the classics she loved as a teenager and her early twenties. She can't bear the thought of going to her grave without having revisited the greatest writers of the age.

She swishes jasmine scented bath foam under the tap and shakes her head, laughing softly at Catherine Morland's foolishness. Why do people blunder on with barely satisfactory lives? Myrah feels impatient with the waste of it all. She thinks of Adrian, then of a man's comments on TV, someone who had survived a horrific rail crash: 'No one on their death bed wishes they'd spent more time at the office.'

Now she's almost on her death bed, Myrah wishes she'd spent more time getting to know herself. Perhaps if in her teens, she'd treated her body with more respect instead of giving it to any boy with a nice body and good line in chat.

Now it's a race against time. She runs downstairs, swings open the fridge, takes out vodka, cranberry juice and pours both into a large tumbler with lots of crushed ice.

Myrah lies in the bath, her mind wandering from Jane Austen's prose to surgeons in masks, severing her breast with a brutality, which startles her. She moans softly, drains her glass and refills it.

Myrah washes her body carefully, thinks maybe if she worships it enough, it will no longer betray her. She fondles her breasts, cherishing the soft skin around her nipples, then frowns when she rediscovers the lump.

If only she'd attended the regular check-ups. If only she hadn't drunk so much and eaten junk food in her teens and twenties. If only she'd been more careful, more respectful. . . If she'd made a different decision twenty years ago. Perhaps she is being punished?

Myrah dresses in a plum coloured satin bra and briefs, pulls on jeans, and a flimsy cotton blouse and resolves to walk and walk until it's time to go and make Adrian's supper. She wants to wallow in the English countryside and let its agelessness seep into her bones.

THE COUNTRY LANE IS ANONYMOUS. Myrah could be anywhere, in any century. The cow parsley tickles her hand as she trails it along beside her. Her nostrils prickle as they sense the oil seed rape flowers in the field behind the hedge. She throws her head back, ignoring the grit stabbing the thin soles of her sandals.

Nothing prepares her for what lies ahead.

Has she lain down on the grass verge to sleep, the long grass stroking her tired legs? Or is this real?

A small girl sits In the middle of the road, playing with a small clump of cowslips. She's picking off the yellow petals one by one and muttering to herself. Her clothes are torn and filthy. Her thin limbs badly bruised and scratched. There are streaks of blood on her thighs. Her face lined with tracks of tears.

Myrah tries to look beyond the bloodshot eyes to see a glimpse of recognition or of hope or relief. Nothing. Her eyes are blank.

As Myrah approaches, the girl makes an effort to stand up, but her legs give way beneath her. Fat tears splash onto the road. Myrah holds out her hand. "What's your name, sweetheart?" Myrah takes a step nearer. "Let me help you up. I won't hurt you." The child trembles and turns her head away. The cowslips and their torn petals are forgotten now. Myrah touches the girl's shoulder and jumps back as the child lets out a howl.

In some ways this is far worse than the dream. At least then there was an obvious reason for the child's distress and dishevelled state. She'd always found her 'dream child' in a war zone.

Myrah doubts her ability to gain the child's trust. "My name's Myrah," she says simply. "Please tell me your name. I'd like to help you." Myrah hopes her voice sounds gentle and kind, yet persuasive.

Still the child remains motionless on the road.

"Why don't I tell you about my dream?" Myrah suggests and sits down on the hot tarmac beside her.

The child frowns at her, looking directly into Myrah's eyes. Myrah hopes the child will see kindness and compas-

sion there; that her instincts will tell her Myrah means
no harm.

They both hear the car at the same moment. Myrah
pulls the girl to her and dashes over the grass verge, her
heart thumping. The girl screams and struggles, as the
battered Peugeot screeches past, full of youths, dance music
pounding out from the stereo. Myrah can feel the child's
thigh pressing against the lump, sending sharp pains
through her upper chest and arm. She finally lets her go.

She wishes she owned a mobile phone, so she could
reach into her handbag and dial for help.

THERE ARE phones ringing all around her now. Mobiles
playing the William Tell Overture, shrill tones of Trim
phones and the old fashioned ringing of clunky olive green
phones with dials.

Myrah wakes in a hospital bed and reaches for the
breast. Her hand touches a dressing, brushes against wires,
and she feels like a bird trapped in fencing.

"The girl?" she asks the room. "What happened to the
little girl?"

A freckle faced nurse smiles at her.

"You're awake, Myrah. That's good. Try and rest."

Myrah looks to the cabinet at the side of the bed and sees
a bottle of Lucozade, bristling in its orange cellophane wrapping, a large arrangement of freesias, arum lilies and chrysan-
themums, but no breast floating in a jar of formaldehyde.

"Where's my breast?" she asks the nurse. "The one they
removed?"

The nurse looks uncomfortable and fiddles with her

watch. Myrah notices her breasts are small, neat and unstartling.

"I wanted to keep it. I told them."

Myrah's voice is fragile like wilting petals of the bell boy weeds she tugged out of the garden, yesterday. Or was it the day before?

"We don't allow that," the nurse states briskly, and begins to plump up Myrah's pillows. "Your husband should be here soon."

Myrah shakes her head. They've got her life neatly sorted and packaged. Unlike her breast, which is probably smouldering away in the hospital incinerator like a perfectly formed twelve week old foetus vacuumed out of a bewildered eighteen-year old.

Myrah watches her husband put his head cautiously round the door of her room.

She sees he's been crying, and wonders whether this time he's been up half the night, sipping treacly Southern Comfort through ice cubes, blaming everyone but himself.

"We'll bear the mental scars of this forever," he said back then, and Myrah wonders if he has a similar platitude for her today.

She asks him to pour her some Lucozade, and as he does so she thinks about those times she was ill in bed as a child, when she held the orange cellophane up to her eyes, revelling in the altered images of her room.

She tries it once more. Orange becomes life on hold for a split second. Then she catches Adrian's frown, and her heart scoops up his misunderstanding. She winces in pain and feels a tear sliding down her cheek.

"Why didn't you tell them?" she asks him. "Why couldn't I keep it this time?"

Myrah, seeing the irritation scud across his eyes like

racing clouds shifting against a gun metal sky, holds the cellophane back up to hers.

The amber tint holds promise.

Sunlight insinuates its way through the blinds, and Adrian shields his eyes. The cellophane catches it, and Myrah sees the rest of her life.

She brings both hands to her stomach.

"New life," she murmurs and lets the cellophane fall at Adrian's feet.

18

PARTY POOPER

A broad shaft of sunlight gilds the water from the horizon to the shore. I listen, as the surging tide sighs heavily onto the beach. The sand feels warm beneath my bare feet, and I squish my toes in its grainy dampness.

It wasn't easy making the decision to move here, but now I wouldn't be anywhere else. It is the perfect place for peace and contemplation.

An elderly couple creak slowly along the shoreline, their scruffy terrier skipping in and out of the water with a piece of driftwood in its mouth. I could never picture Keith and I growing old together. He was always too restless, like a fidgety child.

I turn back to towards the dunes, tufted grass blowing about like a bouffant hairdo. The red-roofed boathouse with its slipway bowing down to the sea looks as if it's on stilts and about to stalk away towards the village, fed-up of being lonely and forgotten.

I think back to Anya's phone call last night. She sounded agitated and annoyed all at the same time.

"Mother's insisting you come down for her birthday. It is her seventieth after all, Rebecca. The whole family's coming. It wouldn't look good, if you were absent. Besides, I'd love to see you. It's been months."

I do feel guilty. Honestly, I do. It's just that.... How can I explain even to myself? I've had enough of other people, I guess. Of being told what to do. There was a time only a few months ago that I seemed to be surrounded by bullies. Colleagues at work badgering me to do this or not to that. Keith nagging about starting a family, despite the fact he wanted to do a six month stint in China - a short-term contract that he felt only he could fulfill. And what about the contract we'd made as a couple in church before God? Didn't that count? He'd promised to be faithful and 'keep thee only unto her', but he'd broken his vow just weeks after our wedding, then couldn't understand why I was so upset.

I can picture the texts and emails as vividly as if they were written in the pale sand. I went to the hotel where they planned to meet and watched as they kissed and fawned over each other next to a fake log fire and a drooping pot plant.

By the time I reach the boat with the navy blue hull leaning drunkenly into the sand, I realise that, not only am I hungry, but desperate for a drink. It seems an age since I sat in a bar, sipping cold Chardonnay and listening in on the locals' conversation. Keith didn't take me to pubs or hotels, only to the cinema or a restaurant. He said he liked evenings at home in front of the TV or in bed with music and a healthy dose of love-making on the side.

The Old Ship Inn ducks down behind the dunes as if it has a guilty secret. It probably has. Smugglers used it a couple of centuries previously and it had probably seen its fair share of secret assignations.

I duck down to avoid the low heavy beams and approach the bar. The chap who runs the local shop is sitting with a pint of Guinness for company. I'd heard his wife died two years ago and that he was broken-hearted.

"Haven't seen you in here before, lass. How's things?"

"Not too bad. Better after a glass of wine, though."

He chuckles and takes refuge in his pint. I'm not sure why people feel awkward around me. I must give off an aura of discontent or intolerance or something they'd prefer not to acknowledge.

I take my wine over to a table by the window and twist round to look at the sea. It sloshes around in the stiff breeze like pewter-coloured soup. I'm hoping for a stunning sunset again this evening, but it looks as if I might be disappointed.

I pick up the plastic menu and decide on the homemade fishcakes and salad. I haven't had a pub meal since before Keith. The girls from work used to organise a weekly get-together at The Bricklayers Arms and we'd eat flaky pastry pies with crispy chips and mushy peas slathered with vinegar. I always looked forward to it. A great way of ending the day.

I haven't seen the girls since I got married. We eventually invited them to the evening reception, but it took me weeks to persuade Keith, who wanted to keep it small and not turn it into some 'shabby party', as he called it.

I flinch. Sometimes images creep in and soil my head. How long will it take to replace those old memories with startling new shiny ones? Maybe I should make more of an effort.

"Can you give me a good reason why you can't come, Rebecca?" Anya asked last night. My sister can be a persistent little madam when she wants to be.

I can give her a reason. Of course, I can. But I won't. I

don't want Mother to find out.

"She's hurting so much, Rebecca. She thinks it's something she's done. No matter how many times I tell her that it's not her fault you left, she won't believe me. If you turned up at the party, then it would make her night. She won't enjoy her evening, unless you're there. You're her first born and have always been her favourite."

I know. And that's a hard burden to carry sometimes. Her expectations of me were always so high. Anya had room to be herself. 'A flighty madam,' Mum always called her, but was secretly proud of Anya's beauty and the way she was at ease with the world. The night Anya came home with a magnum of pink champagne wrapped in rose-coloured cellophane, their mother had burst out laughing.

"Where on earth did you get that? It must have cost a fortune!"

I can picture Anya's broad grin and the way she tapped the side of her nose with her finger. "Don't you worry about that, Mum. Put it in the fridge to cool while I take a nice long soak, then the three of us will drink the lot and toast the fact that life can sometimes be unexpectedly wonderful."

I wish I could be more like Anya. How wonderful to be so carefree and frivolous! No matter how many times I tell myself I'm being silly, I still feel weighed down by what others might be thinking of me. That I'm not worthy, not good enough to be this or do that; never quite making the grade. Yes, I went to university, but only got a Second Class Degree. Yes, I got a good job as a trainee accountant, but left after six months because I was bored. Yes, I wrote a novel, but it never got published, because agents repeatedly told me it wasn't commercial enough. Yes, I married the most handsome man my mother said she'd ever seen, but I couldn't hold onto him.

Stop feeling so bloody sorry for yourself, Rebecca! Sometimes it's Anya's voice admonishing me and others it's my own.

"Ready to order?" asks the pretty waitress who looks like a waif.

I pick up the wine list instead of the menu card. "Yes. Please could I have a bottle of pink champagne and two glasses?"

The waitress looks puzzled, then smiles, "Yes, of course. Would you like to eat?"

"Maybe later."

The shop owner, who always has time for a chat when I buy my daily *Guardian*, looks over and smiles. I suddenly remember his name.

"Will you join me, Barry? I've just ordered champagne."

He blushes and I can see he's struggling to know how to answer.

"Come and sit down. I feel like celebrating."

He walks over, still looking uncertain, as if I'm about to seduce him or worse.

"What are you celebrating, lass?"

The waitress places the ice bucket containing the champagne and two pretty glasses on the table. I pop the cork.

"Life, Barry. I'm celebrating life. Cheers!"

We chink glasses.

I feel sorry that he's going to have to sit and listen to the reasons why I've decided not to go to my mother's birthday party. Still, I figure the alcohol will help, and once we get chatting, he will no longer be able to see the scars that life has etched on my face. And maybe, just maybe, he'll be able to persuade me to forgive my sister for betraying me.

Anya still doesn't know I saw them that night.

19

BROKEN BOWLS AND CAMEL LASHES

The purple blooms on the ceonaphus bobbed in the breeze like pom-poms. Della walked round and round the garden five times before deciding she'd go out today. It had been nine days, ten hours and forty-four minutes since she'd last gone out. The intervals were getting longer and she knew she'd have to do something about that.

Della parked the car and walked over the road to the old graveyard. It couldn't be called that anymore, since there were so few gravestones left. It was more like a park now with squirrels flitting across the stretches of grass and scrambling up the beautiful chestnut trees. The yews still lined the path, as they had when Trinity Church stood here all those years ago. It had been demolished in the 1960s and Della had never found out why.

She sat down on a bench and watched a young man remove his rucksack, place it carefully on the ground, before doing a series of somersaults in the open space beside the old wall. Della applauded his athleticism and bit into an orange, peel and all. She felt she should offer him half for his efforts. He was bound to be thirsty.

"Here, take this. Sorry it's not a whole one," she said, stretching out her palm flat as if she were feeding a horse.

He nodded his head. "Thank you."

He was foreign. Eastern European. Polish, at a guess. There were many Poles living in the town now, working hard to send money back to loved ones and buying the property they never thought they'd own.

Della smiled at the young man and walked away. She'd get her ready meals in M&S, before returning home.

"Madam! Please, wait!"

She stopped walking and turned round.

"I walk with you, please?"

"Have you finished your acrobatics for the day?" she asked him.

"No, not really. I must practise for circus in next town. You come watch?"

Della smiled. "I don't like circuses. Only the camels. I like their long lashes."

The young man nodded. "I am Paul. Not Polish name, but better for work and understanding," he said. "Orange was kind thing. Thank you."

He followed her to the M&S store, chatting in pidgin English about his studies and his job in the circus. He told her about the girl he wanted to marry, but she flew the trapeze and was in love with the man who breathed fire.

Della walked over to the china on display near the front of the store. She wanted to buy her mother a present. She picked up a large bowl with red and purple flowers emblazoned on the inside. Her mother would love it and place it on the dining table in the front room.

"Is rubbish!"

Paul's loud voice ripped through the store and made her jump. Before she had time to realise what was happening, the bowl slipped from her grasp and smashed on the floor of the shop.

There was a collective gasp from the other customers.

"Butterfingers!" shouted Paul at the top of his voice, then began to laugh, clapping loudly.

Della felt the hotness rising from the pit of her stomach. Her cheeks burned and her mouth was dry. She couldn't look up. Her hands were shaking and her legs began to give way. Just as the other shoppers began to clap and cheer, she felt herself drift away.

"I caught you! I save you!" These were the words she heard as the room swam back into focus. "You lucky lady meeting me today. I take you home. Shop won't charge for breakage."

Mortified didn't even begin to cover it. She might have even wet herself a little. How could she face anyone in the store? How could she stop looking at the floor? How she longed to be in her own home, gazing out of the window at her beautiful ceonaphus and the fragile lilac tree!

After what seemed like hours, Della finally looked up to find large forget-me-not blue eyes with camel lashes staring into hers.

"I take you home, lady. I don't know your name."

"Della."

"Pretty name."

And as soon as the words were out of his mouth, Della knew she'd never leave the house again and …. neither would he.

20

MERMAID'S HAIR AND A CARPET OF POPPIES

I stand and gaze at the wild red poppies trampled into the verge. Their red petals remind me of butterfly wings, fragile and vulnerable; a little like me.

She only went to take the rubbish out. An ordinary day in an ordinary suburban street. I hope she didn't have too long to think about what was happening.

They said he had only been out a few hours. Desmond Handy. A forty-year-old man of no fixed abode; a tattoo of an axe on his left arm and another of a black widow spider on his right hand. It didn't take them long to catch him, but it was too late for Suzanne.

She lay in a pool of blood as red as the poppies.

A car goes past and its occupants must think I'm a crazy woman standing by the verge staring at the ground. I can't take my eyes away from the crushed flowers and wonder what trampled them down in their prime on this sunny July day.

It takes me several minutes before I can look up at the denim blue sky again. I pick out faces in the clouds and wish I was lying underneath the huge chestnut tree in the garden instead of exposed and alone on this country lane. But still I walk on until I reach the river bridge. I rest my palms on the warm grey stonework and lean over to look at the water. A skein of dark green weed below the water reminds me of mermaid's hair. Or Suzanne's long straight hair spread out like a fan as she lay on her cape of blood.

We were never close as youngsters. There were too many brothers in between us. I was the eldest and a tomboy. I roamed the village streets with my posse of siblings, for whom Mother said I had to be responsible. In the summer holidays we got up after she'd gone to her office job in the town. I made them breakfast and dressed the little ones. Suzanne wasn't much more than a baby then. I usually took her to Gran's at the opposite end of the village. Suzanne wasn't old enough to share our adventures like lying on our stomachs on the river bank catching minnows in tea strainers or running through the stubble fields after setting fire to some straw. By the time she was old enough, I'd left home to study at Uni in Bath.

The day she was murdered I'd gone round to take her some flowers and a cake I'd made. She'd not long had a miscarriage and was struggling to get over it. Her husband, John, was working abroad for six weeks and couldn't get compassionate leave to come home. She said she could only cope with family.

When I found her, I didn't even check her pulse. There was no point. Why weren't the neighbours gathered round, alerted by her screams? Did she scream? Surely she would have done? Or didn't she even have time to register what was happening?

I walked into her house and the first thing I did was to pick up her Smartphone. There was a voicemail message. I played it six times before I phoned the emergency services. After all, what was the hurry?

Ivy clings to the stonework of the bridge, just as my brothers clung to me when they found out about Suzanne. They were like limpets for weeks afterwards. Once more I trailed around the village with my posse of siblings, but this time the onlookers wore expressions of sympathy, not of annoyance. We weren't up for tying all the door knobs of the terraced cottages together and knocking on the doors.

Today is the first time I've been able to shake them off. This lane is a lane of memories. Only the old elder bushes and hawthorns remember how we were then. The giant willow tree glowering over the water is a youngster; an upstart. It has no idea who I am and why I'm here. I found our initials carved in the stone and trace my fingers through the letters.

I jump with surprise as I feel the lick of a dog's tongue on my bare calf.

"Judy? Is it really you?"

I turn to see Vince, my childhood sweetheart who left the village when his parents moved house in 1976. His face conjures up memories of dried yellow grass and standpipes in the street. That hot shimmering summer where we looked at life through a heat haze wondering if we'd ever seen rain again. I can picture the dark brown cotton print pinafore dress I wore with the ties on the shoulder. It was long and loose and I didn't wear any underwear. I allowed Vince to explore my body underneath its shroud of brown cotton until he excited me too much and I ran home.

He puts an arm around my shoulder. "I heard about Suzanne. I read all the news reports. I can't imagine how you all must be feeling. I didn't make the funeral, sorry. I was in Swansea visiting my girls."

I rest my hand on his. Neither of us are wearing rings. "It's okay, Vince. Don't worry. You're here now."

He hoiks himself up to sit on the bridge and pats the place beside him. I haven't done this since I was sixteen. We sit in silence for a moment and swing our legs. Then he lifts my chin and kisses me on the lips. His kiss takes me back to Fab ice lollies, Kia Ora squash and Fruit Salad sweets.

"Some things don't change, do they, Jude?"

I laugh for the first time since Suzanne died. It feels good. I want to take Vince's hand, lead him down to the water's edge and tear at his clothes. Death has made me hungry for sex. Nostalgia and old memories make me reckless and I pull him from the bridge.

The backs of my legs are riddled with nettle stings afterwards. His dog has run off over the water meadows. Vince calls and whistles for him to come back, as I wipe myself with a dock leaf and pull my clothes back on.

"We can do this again, can't we?" he asks. "Not necessarily here, of course."

It's not until we're walking back over the bridge that I look back to where we lay and see the carpet of crushed wild poppies we must have been lying on.

Was my hair splayed out against the scarlet background just as Suzanne's had been? Was my panting in ecstasy an echo of her fear?

"Stop thinking about it, Jude. Come back to my place for a drink. I think we both need one."

I'd forgotten the way Vince has always seemed to know what I need and when.

"I'm glad you moved back to the village, Vince. I think I might need you."

As we walk down the lane, I think back to that voicemail message on Suzanne's phone.

I need to see you, Suzy. One last time before John comes back. Please, babe.

At first I was shocked to recognise his voice; a voice that took me back to Fab lollies and Fruit Salad; to dried yellow grass and standpipes, but after I'd listened to it a few times, part of me was glad that Suzanne had been able to share a bit of my past after all.

FLICKING NAILS

There are surfers here riding the gentle waves, and I'm temporarily blinded by the vastness of blue sea splattered with shards of diamonds. The rocks are jagged, pointed and zigzag down the beach in haphazard shapes.

"I would take the moon out of the sky for you," my father said last night.

It was his way of trying to reassure me. Just the way he always used to, in fact. Except back then, words spoke louder than his actions. He scarpered with a woman from the soap factory when I was four, and I didn't see him again till I was twelve, when he decided to turn up at the house with a bunch of garage flowers for my mother and a bag of sweets for me.

A boy sits on the sand and flicks rusty nails at a cluster of pebbles. Every now and then he looks up towards the horizon and shades his eyes from the sun.

"I'm proud you're a mother now, Helen," my father told me last night.

Not that he had ever seen my two children. We'd

arranged to meet at the small B&B on the promenade where I had a single room. Dad was staying at The Grosvenor down the road. Lucy, the soap factory woman, was history. He was now shacked up with a wealthy woman called Eunice who owned a golf course in Spain.

"You'd like her," he promised last night. "The two of you should meet."

I don't think so. I have no desire to meet any of the women my father has had affairs with over the years. Has he forgotten what these women did to my mother? When I told my father about mother's hoarding, a pained expression bubbled up under his smooth tanned face.

"She always did have trouble throwing anything away," he said.

Not like you, I thought. How easy it was for him to cast aside his family, his friends, his whole life.

Always moving on to the next dream; the next woman.

"We only hear the lies we deserve," my father confided last night.

He went on to explain that people like my mother who didn't make any effort in life had what was coming to them. Deceit, betrayal, disloyalty. I think that was the point I slapped him.

I turn my back on the sea view and see a dot of a man herding a zillion sheep up a grassy hill. My stomach flips when I remember the wool my mother gathered around her. Balls and balls of two, three and four ply in supermarket carrier bags, dotted all around her house. You couldn't see the floor in any of the rooms, except the kitchen. But it wasn't just wool she collected. Hundreds and thousands of ornaments. Ainsley, Wedgwood, assorted china, glassware. She bought them from various charity shops all over the scruffy little town she lived in. Most of this tat was in boxes.

A few items were displayed on wobbly teak shelves or units. She had a beautiful glass fronted display cabinet, given to her by an old aunt who had moved into a care home. It housed some of the best pieces of china Mother bought, but now it was hidden away behind a tottering pile of cardboard boxes filled with ornaments wrapped in yellowing newspaper.

My mother had built herself a fortress of clutter to cocoon herself inside when she could no longer face the big bad world. The security she craved, she provided with her possessions.

There's a stiff breeze and my hair flaps in my face.

"You need to get it cut," my father said last night. "A smarter style. I'll pay."

He didn't understand my purple and pink leggings with the swirly pattern; the oversized Tibetan cardigan in psychedelic colours; the electric blue Dr Marten boots.

"Middle-aged hippy," he'd muttered last night.

The small boy has finished with the nails and he's busy collecting them up in a small bundle. He stuffs them in the pocket of his shorts. He looks across at me before stumbling back up the dunes to wherever it is he's going on a sunny Saturday afternoon.

It's time to go back to the B&B to change for dinner. I have bought a dress today. A shift dress in cotton. It's rather plain and dowdy, but it will make my father happy.

I'm just about to walk back up the beach, following in the small boy's footsteps, when my mobile phone rings.

"Helen? It's your mother," says Sally, the next-door-neighbour. "You'd better get over here as quickly as you can. She's had a fall."

The call I've been dreading has finally come. How often have we warned her, my husband and I, how dangerous it is to have all those carrier bags and boxes on the stairs?

"She'll break her neck one day," my father predicted last night. "Still, we all get the death we deserve."

A seagull skims past my head and screeches a warning, but I'm too lost in thought as I step out into the road. The last thing I hear is the clatter of nails hitting the tarmac and the cry of a small boy.

22

SOUNDS OF DARKNESS

Until my last wife, I was happy.

Until my last wife I drank four pints of Adnam's ale every night in The Old Ship Inn. I'd then amble out into the night and watch the pewter-coloured sea roll and heave like an old drunk.

"Lean into me, old friend. We can beat the wind," I say to Arthur, who has been in the pub since five.

The beach has virtually disappeared and what's left of it is uninviting; too wet, too grey, too slippery.

The old and the ancient emerge from the dusk. The Victorian hotels frown down upon the beach like proud patricians.

We light a fire on the beach. When it dies and night sweeps over us, we move on, staggering like old tramps towards the town.

"Listen!" says Arthur and stops us both dead in our tracks. "Hear that? That, my boy, is the sound of darkness going."

I nod sagely. "Yeah, man. Darkness. Always goes eventually," I say weaving my way along the main road.

"Fancy a last one in The Dungeness?" Arthur asks, fishing in his pockets for the last of his cash.

I grin. "Sure thing."

We approach the bar. The landlady gives us a look that could kill. She's about to call last orders.

"What's it to be?"

We order whiskies and carry them to a table near the window and sit in silence before knocking them back in one hit.

Each summer, every summer, last summer. It's the same routine.

We go back to Arthur's flat. It's not sex, nor love, although body fluids are involved. It satisfies. It's good.

Later, much later, I stagger out into the dawn, before the beach tractors trundle down the sand ready for the day's work.

One man sings, another man cries.

23

COWBOYS AND INDIANS

The woman in the seat opposite has too many teeth. They are crammed into her tiny mouth like boulders on a mountainside. There is bound to be a landslip or subsidence at some point.

When they told me later that her name was Arlene McGovern, I wept. I'm not sure why. Knowing her name made it more personal somehow.

If I'd have known, I'd have whispered to her, "You have sixty seconds…" and then she'd have done something more significant in her last few moments than just continue to read her *Metro* newspaper.

I wonder what happened to those teeth? Did they explode from her mouth and pierce the flesh of the other passengers in the same way a piece of the bomber's shin bone speared Tom Davidson's left eye?

The image makes me think about the time I was six-years-old, wearing pale blue cotton shorts my mother had made on her Singer sewing machine. Stevie and Kate had tied me to a target in the middle of Stevie's lawn. I was always the Indian. They ran around the garden with their toy guns and garden canes sharpened into spears. I can still feel the warmth and the wetness, as urine soaked my shorts in the split second before Stevie threw the spear which broke the flesh of my eyelid. I remember the shock of the blood spilling onto my legs and the fact I couldn't see a thing until Stevie's mum carefully wiped the blood away with a dark green flannel.

She had to wait for his dad to come home from work before she could take me to A&E. I watched as he threw Stevie face down on the bed in their bungalow and slid off his leather belt. I turned away, but couldn't shut out Stevie's screams as the belt met the flesh of his bare buttocks. I wanted to rush into that bedroom and rescue him, but was too scared.

The man next to me is wearing a black-tie and inappropriate clothing for an eight o'clock commute. Perhaps he's only just returning from a formal dinner the night before. Has he spent the night with a woman, nestled in her arms amongst warm, semen-stained sheets until the alarm on his phone told him it was time to leave for work?

When I come round after the blast I can see his black-trousered leg hanging from a bent piece of metal near the ceiling. His highly polished shoe is still attached to his foot. I remember thinking how impossible that seemed.

I don't know why we've agreed to do this documentary. The production company assured us from the start that they'd only film our head and shoulders. We simply had to talk to camera about our experiences. It was easy to reel off the account of that morning as I'd done a thousand times before. It was like pressing 'Play' - the words spilling out automatically like the lyrics of a well-known song.

Black-tie man said he couldn't face The Tube anymore. His hour-long commute began and ended that day. He didn't tell us where he'd spent that night, but it was obvious that it wasn't at home. His name is Brian and I'm happy that I can ignore the wheelchair and the image of his severed leg hanging from the ceiling when I kiss him on the cheek and wish him well.

I've acquired a liking for cheese and piccalilli sandwiches on M&S Seeded Bread. My hands are usually covered in ink when I eat my lunch. After what I've been through, it doesn't bother me much. My job in the print shop continues much as before, except now I take a bus instead of the Tube. It's when I get home that the nightmare begins all over again. Sitting in my flat, eating my dinner alone and listening to the radio. Memories of how Andy and I planned our engagement party over a bottle of Shiraz, listening to Coldplay on the stereo. The nights we spent snuggled up in bed watching old episodes of *Seinfeld* and gossiping about our friends. The chaotic dinner parties we used to go to in Camden; the pub bands and drinking ice cold beer. Always getting the last Tube home. What a huge part in our lives that Line played.

Tom Davidson is the only one amongst us who continues to commute in exactly the same way as he did that summer's day.

"I won't let the bastards get the better of me," he says.

His words sound hollow. I'm sure he shivers with nerves as he stands on the platform each morning.

"It can't happen twice in one lifetime," he says, and I can almost see him crossing his fingers behind his back.

I gained more than I lost that day in July 2005. I picture the bracelet with the silver snakes entwined like lovers, glowing white hot on the tracks, shot through the floor like poor Stan whose family agreed to appear on the programme with us. His son seems to have taken a bit of a liking to me.

He's cute, but he must be ten years younger and lives too far away to make him a viable prospect.

The fact that I can even think about another relationship after Andy is a vast step forward. He visited me once in hospital, but his eyes kept sliding away from my face, as if he couldn't see beyond the bandages. My eyes implored him to look into them a little more deeply than he would have done otherwise, but he simply turned away and addressed the bottle of Lucozade on the bedside cabinet. He told the dimpled bottle that he was very busy at work - a new contract that would take him abroad for much of the year. He told it that it was regretful that such a lucrative offer had come at a time like this. The bottle stood to attention when he begged its forgiveness and said that he wasn't abandoning it, honest, Julie.

I didn't cry when he left the ward. I've become so much more accepting.

Arlene McGovern with too many teeth was a violin teacher. I imagine her pupils sniggering whenever she turned her back, making jokes about tombstones.

Poor Arlene. They told me she was due to be married in the August. Her sister said that they couldn't even bury her in the beautiful wedding dress she'd bought two weeks previously. They hadn't got a whole body to fit it onto.

I think about Stevie and Kate and me, the sitting target.

Cowboys and Indians. That's all it comes down to at the end of the day.

CUCKOO SPIT

G nats dance above our heads as Ken dithers over whether he needs his raincoat or not. Such a simple decision, yet he's struggling.

As I watch him pace alongside our car, I wonder why the decision to pursue Daisy Collins was such an easy one.

"I'll tie it round my waist," he says to no-one in particular. "Better have it just in case. A good year for the garden, but a devil for us walkers, eh?"

I nod my head and smile.

I squint in the sunlight as I look over to the burnished beige wheat fields and think about when we first met. I was singing with a folk band at an open air gig in the park. Ken was leaning against a tree trunk, smoking a roll-up; his leather hat tipped forward over his eyes. I couldn't tell whether he was looking at me or not. He caught up with me 'backstage', in other words, at the back of the bandstand and he told me I sang like a Celtic goddess.

"Ready?" he asks now. "We'll get a great view from the top of that hill. St Andrew's Church is particularly striking. It's shaped rather like a rocket, don't you think? I mean, I wonder what the ancients had seen and what inspired them to create tall spires pointing at the sky. Monkeys imitate what they've seen, you know."

My mind wanders as Ken explains the complicated theory he'd read about in one of his geeky magazines. I feel sorry for his students. I can imagine them texting secretly under their desks as Ken paces the classroom mulling over bizarre theories before asking their opinion. I'm so glad I was never his pupil.

He's leaning on the stone bridge, flicking stones into the water as if he has all the time in the world.

"Yes, I'm ready, honey," I tell him, hitching my rucksack up on my back and checking the laces of my walking boots.

"We should be back by about seven. Does that suit you?"

"Fine."

Ours is an easy relationship. We've both mellowed over the past fifteen years. I had a temper to match my red hair and until recently was plagued by vile PMT and paranoia at certain times of the month. Ken bore my moods with patience, but several times we rowed about the nights he stayed up marking into the wee small hours or the nights he gave private tuition in other people's houses.

This indigo blue sky is perfect for lovers to walk along remote country footpaths and let their feelings play amongst the reeds and wild poppies. But we're no longer lovers and it hurts.

I glance down at a glob of cuckoo spit clinging pathetically to a nettle. That's me. Clinging to the nastiest weed, which has no qualms about dishing out pain to those who get too close.

We reach the top of the hill. I'm surprised that Ken is panting a little, as he's usually so fit.

"There, see that spire?" he asks, pointing to the horizon.

"Beautiful piece of architecture. Fancy getting married in a church like that."

I shoot him a look. It's such an uncharacteristic remark.

Heads of wheat bob their heads as we pass. I listen to the combines rumbling in the distance, knowing the harvest will soon be over for another year as the nights start drawing in and the wheat is baled up in barns. Then I look at Ken.

He's studying the Ordnance Survey Map. He looks older. His skin has taken on the greyish hue normally present on the faces of heavy smokers. He has a slight paunch, which was never there before. I try to think back to when I last saw my husband naked. I gulp back a surprising rush of tears when I realise I can't remember.

We've left the wheat fields behind now and skirt along the edge of a lush meadow. Clover flowers with petals like desiccated coconut cover the ground and a grey horse is grazing near a line of burly oak trees.

At one time we'd have been holding hands and laughing. Ken would have pushed me against the broad tree trunk, the bark brushing my bare thighs and he'd have kissed me hard, sliding his hands down the back of my shorts.

We used to make love anywhere and everywhere. We were good together.

That was before Daisy Collins.

They didn't call her that in the papers. The locals referred to her as 'The Britney Girl', because she had those stupid bunches like the singer in the *Hit Me Baby One More Time* video. The press blamed her. Said she dressed provocatively and led him on. Her school clamped down hard on uniform afterwards and insisted the girls wore their skirts on or below the knee. They were told to wear tights, not socks. Make-up was banned.

I saw Daisy Collins last week in Morrison's. I thought we'd moved far enough away, but they obviously use the same out-of-town supermarket. I'm surprised her parents haven't moved to a different part of the country. I wonder if Ken has seen Daisy here, too. He has so much time on his hands now, I often get him to do the shopping. He was lucky to get even a part-time post afterwards. If it wasn't for that clever barrister he'd be serving a jail sentence. Quite how he shrugged the whole thing off, I can't imagine. The man in court wasn't the Ken I knew. He'd changed.

"Did you find that book you were looking for yesterday, love?" he asks as we cross a road, the tar melting and sticky beneath our feet.

One of my favourite novels. *Crow Lake* by Mary Lawson. I thought I'd lent it to a friend who'd forgotten to give it back, but I found it nestling in a box we hadn't unpacked since the move. I took it out with a little whoop of joy and that wonderful sense of anticipation that comes with knowing you're going to be spending the next few hours in the company of characters you've grown to love. It was like opening a brand new box of your favourite chocolates.

Then I saw the envelope. It was lying at the bottom of the box. I could tell exactly what was inside by the weight of it and the shape.

Photographs.

Why had he been so damn careless? Why hadn't he hidden them more carefully?

"Yes, Ken, I did find the novel. I read it in one sitting."

The glowering shadows of the oak trees cover the width of the road and there's grass growing down the middle. Our footsteps seem to echo around us.

I can still see the naked images of Daisy Collins flash before my eyes. One of her looking coy as she glances behind her, one hand splayed across her left buttock.

And then the other girl whose name I didn't know. She lay spreadeagled on a bed with a gold satin coverlet. Her eyes stared at the ceiling as if something she saw up there surprised her. Her skin was pale; too pale. A miniscule trickle of blood in the corner of her mouth tainted her otherwise perfect face.

"I found the photos, Ken. Yesterday when I was looking for my book."

Musky scents invade my nostrils as we walk through a glade of thick foliage. Elder bushes and ground plants with leaves like paddles brush our legs as we pass. Nature is too close for comfort here and all I can see is green.

"Good, Cassie. That's good you found them. I wanted you to know."

And now I'm the one with decisions to make. Unlike Ken, my mind is easily made up.

Red petals like butterfly wings peep shyly from the long grass on the edge of the copse.

I turn to look behind me and Ken is holding out his hand, tears rolling down his cheeks.

25

I LIKE YOUR BOW-TIES, MR DAY!

D avey was haunted by the question. It crept into his dreams like spikes on barbed wire. It stabbed his bare legs and prickled his ear lobes. Day-in, day-out he lived with the question. His vision was obscured by the bold question mark hovering on the horizon. It followed him wherever he went.

"Davey? Are you daydreaming again?" his teacher would ask, waving his Maths exercise book in front of his face like a drooping flag.

"Sorry, Miss," he'd reply.

Davey was always sorry. He knew when to apologise. His mother told him he was a polite, sensible boy.

"Davey, aren't you going to clean your plate?" his mother asked most days.

The question had blunted his appetite. It snaked between the pink clematis which covered the garden fence, the apple tree and the pergola like a blanket of snow. The question made him thirsty for fresh water in a mountain stream.

"Davey, you won't be late again, will you?" the newsagent

asked yesterday morning. "I'm running out of patience and there are other boys who'd happily do your job."

Davey hated upsetting people, especially adults. He didn't do it on purpose, but he seemed to have a knack for it.

The question had punctured his bike tyres and wormed its way around the handlebars, curling through his bike chain and tripping him up every time he put his feet down at a road junction.

"Davey, do you love me?"

The question slithered into his thoughts when he was singing along to his favourite Queen song. *Don't Stop Me Now* was the best record he'd ever bought. He played it over and over in the bedroom with the mauve painted walls and the brown skirting boards his mother cleaned with Vim.

"Davey, you have to choose," his grandmother told him every Saturday when he went for tea.

She gave him pikelets dripping with butter and strong tea with three sugars in a dainty cup, which was special, because it was part of her Royal Albert china set. He loved its fragile pale blue colour and the delicate ferns painted on by someone with a steady hand. Sometimes him and Nanna had Welsh Rarebit, which was just cheese on toast, his dad said on one of his rare visits.

"Do you love me, Davey? It's a simple question."

Sometimes he'd stay the night at Nanna's, lying awake in the rickety bed with the heavy electric blanket in the draughty room at the back, trying to digest the fatty food he had for tea and hoping the cheese wouldn't make him have bad dreams.

"Choose, Davey. You haven't much time left, son."

Which one to choose?

It wasn't like trying to decide between Spangles and Opal Fruits or between *The Dandy* and *The Beano*.

"Do you love me, Davey? Do you?"

He loved them both. So, so much. How could he decide? His mother and her floral pinny, baking his favourite chocolate cake and giving him the best birthday party ever with the matching green glasses and jug for the squash. Or his father in his green galoshes, patting him on the back when he caught his first fish and taking him to the chippy for his tea.

"Who do you want to live with, Davey? It's up to you."

But he didn't want it to be up to him. Why couldn't they choose? Why couldn't that nice lady in the black car choose? Or Mr Merriman, the newsagent? Or Miss Clough, his Maths teacher?

His mum loved watching Question Time on TV. It was a new programme. Davey couldn't understand the appeal. A panel of people arguing and trying to decide which party was best and who should be Prime Minister with people jeering in the audience. Still, perhaps they could decide who he lived with?

Davey tried to block out The Big Question, which seemed to be growing bigger by the minute. The tall, bold question mark that stood in his way, as he picked up his new Parker pen and the notepad he'd bought with his paperboy wages from Mr Merriman.

Dear Mr Day, I like those bow-ties you wear. I was wondering....

26

CHASTE KISS CHASE

The tang of salty air hit them as they stepped out of The Ship Inn. It was dusk; the sun slipping behind the horizon in a slither of orange.

They ran round the pub car-park like lunatics. Dom pulling at her cardigan, which she shrugged off like shedding skin.

"That's cheating," he gasped. He was red in the face from cider and exertion. "I had you then!"

"Can't catch me!" she taunted and dodged behind a black BMW.

She held her breath. Where was he? Then, "Boo!". She shrieked and laughed, then he held her tightly and kissed her on the lips. When she finally pulled away from him, she realised she couldn't unlock her gaze from his.

"Let's watch the sunset," he said and took her hand. They walked slowly, their arms wrapped around each other as they headed towards a wooden bench, badly weathered by years of crashing waves and strong westerly winds.

The figures on the pier in the distance were like those from a Lowry painting.

"Happy?" he asked.

She turned and they leapt into each other's eyes once more.

"Of course. Never happier." She didn't dare say anymore.

"Just friends, though," he reiterated. "We can't be anything other than that."

"I know," she said and squeezed his hand.

She watched the cars like Dinkey toys climbing the hairpin bend to her right. The sea's shushing like a lullaby rocking her to sleep.

"I could stay here forever like this, Dom."

"You might get cold," he quipped, the creases around his eyes deepening as he smiled at her.

"We could always play kiss chase again."

"We could. We could, but we shouldn't. We had an agreement, remember?"

Isabel nodded and looked down at her wedding ring. She began to twist it round and around her finger. She felt cross with herself as tears sprang up and spilled over, dribbling down her cheeks as if they had a mind of their own. It was so hard keeping her side of the bargain.

"Let's walk along the beach," he suggested. "I haven't got much time left."

He held out his left hand, naked of rings and she took it. It was a large hand. He had big fingers with square tips and strong white nails, trimmed back short. She felt the callouses and smiled. It was a hand that had held hers only recently, yet she felt as if it had been holding her steady for years.

Huntcliff Nab loomed up ahead like a Victorian lady lifting her skirts to paddle in the water.

"Ten minutes and I'll have to turn back," he said. "It's a long journey. The boys have probably wrecked the house by now. I'll get back to find empty beer cans and a lounge full of drunken eighteen-year-olds eating pizza and playing Deadzone 3."

"You love it really," she said, unable to tear her eyes away from his. "Will we do this again, friend?"

She could feel his fingers twist her wedding ring. "Maybe. It doesn't feel right. Kez is my best mate, after all."

"I thought I was," she said, biting back more tears.

"You both are. That's the trouble," he said, biting his thumb nail.

Pinpricks of light seemed to spring up around them, signalling the end of the day. The beach tractors surrounding them, sulky and abandoned, as Dom and Isabel turned back towards the town.

"One last game of kiss chase!" he said and began to run.

Unable to resist, Isabel ran after him, laughing more than she had in years. Living in the moment. That was what mattered. They ran around in circles on the beach until she was dizzy. Collecting her prize was all that mattered. That one last kiss and she'd never know if there'd be another. A chaste kiss as befitted best friends.

The old and the new emerged from the dusk; the sea a nagging voice, encroaching on Isabel and Dom, urging them to part.

And when Isabel got back to the flat, Kez was in the hall-way, looking out of the window.

"You've been gone for ages," he said, just as hard bullets of hail hit the glass.

"I got back just in time," she replied, leaning over him. "I hadn't got a coat. Stupid weather can't make its mind up."

Kez didn't look at her. He simply wheeled the chair back and headed towards the living room. Just as he reached the door, he stopped, turned and in that irritatingly dismissive way of his, said, "I saw you, Isabel."

Her heart plunged through the wooden floor and she leant against the sturdy window frame for support.

She heard the swell of voices from the TV set and sank to her knees. Isn't this what you wanted? she asked herself. To change your life. To move on.

But how could she choose between them? And Dom wouldn't have her; wouldn't betray his boyhood friend.

"Duty before pleasure," her mother had reminded her on her last visit. "Adults who play games have to face the consequences."

One game of kiss chase, that's all it was, Isabel told herself, pulling at a loose thread on the hem of her top. No harm done.

She stood back up and turned to the window. The sea was now an angry, toxic mix of spray and foam. She thought of Dom driving back down the motorway, the windscreen battered by hailstones as fat as marbles, wipers making no impact, lorries streaming by and buffeting his small car like dinosaurs' tails side-swiping a sloth, and wondered once more if their afternoon at the beach was to be their last.

"Isabel?" Kez's gentle voice, coaxed her back to the present.

Her mouth was so dry, she found it almost impossible to reply.

"Yes, honey?"

"I love you."

27

JELLY TOTS AND SPANGLES

He's pathetic really, standing at the till in Lidl with his four cans of cheap 4% lager and a single carrier bag.

"Shaken, not stirred," he says and holds onto my solitary bottle of red wine I'm buying to replace the one Sam broke earlier.

I notice his hands are shaking and he speaks as if he's had a stroke. The whites of his eyes have that tell-tale yellowish tinge and there's a packet of rolling tobacco in his trouser pocket.

I can tell he's taken a bit of a shine to me. He obviously doesn't remember who I am. We're poles apart these days.

I watch him as he shuffles out of the shop, no doubt eager to quench his thirst. I know he'll down those four cans as if they contained water. Then he'll open the bottle of vodka he has at home and won't go to bed till it's all gone.

Damien. It's been about twenty-five years.

We played together as children. The height of our decadence a packet of jelly tots from the corner shop. We ran, laughed and tumbled down grassy hills and the metal slide in the park. We played kiss chase and hide n' seek. We once stole a packet of Spangles and scoffed them down as fast as we could before Mr Jackman, the newsagent, caught us.

Later it was two litre bottles of cider in the park, sitting on the roundabout or the swings, smoking and drinking and pretending we were adults.

It wasn't until we shared a flat in Kenwood Grove that things started to get out of hand. First it was weed, then skunk. All the time we were washing our cares away with vodka and coke.

Damien lost his job first. He earned a decent wodge as a bricklayer and even did a month's stint in Germany. Very *Auf Wiedersehen Pet*. Things changed fast then. I struggled to get out of bed to do the early shift at the biscuit factory and stopped going to night school.

When Damien brought a friend called Fraser back to the flat, I called it a day. Fraser was a dealer - a heroin dealer.

I get home and place the bottle of wine on the worktop. I'll wait for Sam to get in before I open it. I know that one large glass while preparing dinner can easily turn into two before Sam has even had chance to take a sip.

I slip off my black jacket and roll up my shirt sleeves. I'm trying a new recipe tonight. A Moroccan dish, which I hope will remind Sam of our holiday.

I pull the tiny red elastic band from the bunch of spring onions and Damien worms his way back into my thoughts. I can almost taste the orange Spangles and feel the brittle crunch of the sweets between my teeth. Next thing I know, I'm crying.

Sam comes home to find me huddled up on the kitchen sofa with a glass of red and a box of tissues. He doesn't say a word. He simply comes over and holds me close.

"Bad day at work? Someone you knew?"

I shake my head. "No, it wasn't work. I saw Damien in the supermarket."

"Ah. Want to talk about it?"

I shake my head. "I should get on with the dinner. I'm trying something different."

Sam smiles, then gets up to pour himself a glass of wine.

My heart has gone out of cooking the dish. I sling in the ingredients willy-nilly without checking the recipe properly, sloshing in a good dash of Merlot as I go.

"Why don't you go up and change out of your work clothes while that simmers, honey?" Sam suggests. "You still smell of death."

Sam hates me working at the funeral parlour, but it's a good steady job with no shortage of clientele. Today we did a middle-aged woman (heart attack), a very overweight man (huge coffin) and baby twins.

In the bedroom I pull on tracksuit bottoms and a pale pink cami top. I sit on the bed and stare at my face in the mirror. This is the face Damien once held between his hands and promised to love forever and ever. At nineteen I truly believed we'd never part. We made plans for two kids and a cottage on the cliff road. We planned holidays abroad and camping with the kids at Glastonbury. The nearest we got to any of those things was buying two sleeping bags when the bed broke and we couldn't afford to replace it.

Living by the sea meant we didn't have to go outside of Weston for our fix of salt water and beach. A jellyfish washed ashore once and Damien lay on the sand and blew smoke in its face, the sunlight casting a strip of sparkling diamonds across the water.

Why didn't he recognise me today? I realise this is what hurts most.

Yes, my hair is cut short. I wear a suit instead of skimpy

shift dresses or shorts. I'm a couple of stones heavier. But he should have recognised those eyes he gazed into so many times.

I go back downstairs to dish up, something niggling away at my sub-conscious like a nibbling fish in a bucket.

At work the next day I pick up the agenda for the day. Two at St. Matthews, four to the Crem, one at the private eco-friendly burial ground run by a hippy farmer.

"Had a new one in early hours," says Rufus. "Me and Dev went to pick him up. An old alkie from the flats down by Lidl."

I snap around to face him. I feel the colour drain from my face. He doesn't need to tell me the name. I know.

"Family are coming in this afternoon."

"Family?"

"Yeah, a wife and a son, apparently."

Not Damien then, surely? I hadn't pictured him living with anyone. A shambling, lonely druggie/alcoholic who'd destroyed every relationship he ever had.

"The wife's a Mrs Simpson," says Rufus, checking his notes. "Will you see her? Woman's touch and all that."

I have to. I need to put myself through the torture of asking the woman Damien Simpson married those necessary questions like what she wanted him to wear and what did she want to do about his wedding ring.

At lunchtime I walk to the nearest shop and buy a packet of jelly tots. I'll tuck them into his coffin before they screw down the lid, because they don't make Spangles anymore.

28

BLACK JACKS AND SPARROWS

Penny walks around with a pocket full of sparrows. They're only half alive - or half dead, whichever way you want to look at it.

Everyday she visits Mrs Sherman's corner shop and buys five liquorice bootlaces and ten Black Jacks, then she kisses dirty-faced boys poking her black tongue inside their mouths.

The day she decides to go 'all the way' with Sam Trimlett is the day one of the sparrows falls out of her pocket. Penny sees it as an omen. It's dead, of course, so she buries it next to the slide in Coffrey Park. She makes a small wooden cross from two ice lolly sticks and carefully writes the name 'Olly' on the horizontal stick with a black felt tip she pinched from Mrs Sherman's.

Sam Trimlett has waxy ears and bitten down nails. He farts a lot and lives on chips from Friar Tuck's. Penny decides that he'll be the boy with the biggest dick. She heard her mother telling Donna next door that size *did* matter and next time she'd choose a bloke with 'a big 'un'. Still, it wouldn't hurt to line up the dirty-faced boys under the canal bridge with their trousers and pants round their ankles. Better to be safe, than sorry.

Sam Trimlett's sole is hanging off his shoe and at first she can't bring herself to look at his dick. All six of the dirty-faced boys have an erection. They scuffle and giggle and taunt Penny, asking which one of them she wanted first and which one would be last in line. They make jokes about sloppy seconds, but Penny knows that all six of them are gagging for it and she alone has the power to decide who she'll allow to go all the way and who'd have to make do with a wank as they watch.

Adam Smith's dick is bent over slightly to one side like a banana. Somehow she finds this fascinating and she wants to know what it will feel like inside her. Poor Charley Rowe's is miniscule; thin and weedy, a bit like him. She's pleased to see that as she'd suspected, Sam's is the biggest by a good inch. Still, she can't help wondering about Adam's.

"You and you!" she says, pointing to Adam and Sam.

Which one first? She waits until the other dirty-faced boys have pulled up their trousers and pants.

"You lot can piss off. And no looking!" she says, even though she knows they will. It all adds to the excitement she feels.

Penny's already decided to take Sam Trimlett aboard the disused narrowboat which is moored a few feet away. She takes his left hand, as he holds up his trousers with the other. He isn't wearing underpants and he's sweating slightly, despite a fresh autumn breeze. She expects him to have a grin on his face, but he looks more worried than anything. Probably his first time.

Adam Smith seems unsure what to do.

"Wait there," she tells him and points down at the towpath with its coating of dead leaves.

She knows he'll turn his back and put his fingers in his ears, because he doesn't want to lose it before he's used it.

Penny leads Sam to the bowels of the boat. It smells musty and damp. Dust motes dance in front of the cobwebbed windows. Most of the fixtures and fittings have long since gone, but someone has thoughtfully left a stained mattress behind. She wonders how many boys and men have left their mark on the navy and white ticking.

PENNY TAKES off her grey and torn jacket, the sparrows still in the pocket, their wings clipped and still, and lays it on the dusty wooden floor. Next she removes her pale green knickers and tosses them casually onto the jacket, before hitching up her dirty cream dress and lying down on the mattress.

Sam's knees are trembling and he seems unsure what to do next. Penny reaches for him and takes both his hands, then pulls him down beside her. There are no sounds apart from his rapid breathing and the quacking of ducks. The sparrows are too weak now even to cheep in protest.

A solitary drip of sweat slides down Sam's cheek and onto Penny's pale thigh. She smiles, takes his grubby fingers and pushes them inside her. Then she slowly withdraws the fingers, now slick with her juices, then holds them under his nose, then pushes them into his mouth. Sam looks faintly disgusted, but his excitement takes over. Penny shakes her head. She has the power and she will decide what happens next.

"Hold your fuckin' horses, Sam. You're as bad as the rest," she tells him, before taking his dick in her hand. She likes the way it pulses with life and can't wait to feel it throbbing inside her.

She guides him carefully in. She's more than ready for him.

Sam moves rapidly up and down. He feels bigger than he looks and Penny smiles, then turns her head to watch one of the sparrows as its head lists to one side, its life over.

Sam cries out at the end and she clutches his bare buttocks hard, as she rocks to her own sweet end. She can taste liquorice tinged with the metallic taste of blood and she realises she's bit her own cheek.

One sparrow left.

Penny shoos Sam out of the boat and beckons Adam towards her.

29

POMPEII 1972

J umpin' Jacks lie like coiled worms on the rickety camping table underneath the kitchen window.

Mum is wrapping jacket potatoes in tin foil ready to put on the dying embers of the bonfire, and Dad is lighting the Catherine Wheel. The Standard Firework box is almost empty. There's just the Mount Vesuvius, a cone-shaped firework Dad always saves till last; a Spitfire and a Flying Saucer.

I hope Toby arrives in time for the Jumpin' Jacks. I love the way they chase us round the lawn.

"Come and grate some cheese for the potatoes, Diane!" Mum shouts.

It's only when I'm through the back door that I hear a whistle from the garage. Toby must be hiding. He's four years older than me and teases me all the time. Last week he set up his army play-tent in the kitchen and said he'd give me a tenner if I showed him my privates. I hid the brown note in a pink Tupperware box in our pantry. Mrs Crowther still hasn't asked for it back.

I grate the cheese, then skulk off to find Toby. He's sitting on an oil drum holding a lit sparkler. It's dangerous and thrilling at the same time. Just the two of us in the garage with the fireworks.

"Which one shall we light first?" he asks with a grin.

I point with a trembling finger, then run.

We never did see the Jumpin' Jacks. When Mount Vesuvius erupted, Toby turned to ash.

30

THE CLEANSING

I'm slipping off the edge, gripping the mud as he thrusts. As I twist his blonde curls in my fingers I wonder why I'm here doing this with him.

It must be the gold. Liquid Gold. Ian shoved the tiny bottle under my nose, told me to take a big sniff. Wham. Makes you feel horny, he said. He was right about that.

I breathe in the early morning smells and open my eyes to see a watery sun catching the dew on the water meadows. I suck in those earthy scents; the moss and ripe vegetation. I open my ears to the sounds of water rushing under the stone bridge and allow Ian to take me with him. Our orgasm is one. A spectacular feat considering I'm so fucked up about Joe.

Ian and I have enjoyed many furtive couplings, daring others to discover our secret passion. Ian has a sense of adventure. We've done it all over the place; in my parents' conservatory while they slept in their respectable twin beds; against someone's 4x4 in the Red Lion car-park and once in the Ladies toilet of The Miners Arms. Joe would never have contemplated it. I picture his dark head on a feather-filled pillow and an involuntary muscle spasm grips Ian tighter.

We both giggle uncontrollably as we shimmer down from the dizzy heights of orgasm. I feel Ian's penis sliding down and out. I feel soggy, sated and superior.

I turn onto my stomach and look over to the crushed grass footpath we've made from the wooden gate. I feel mud ingrained in my nails. Then I look to my left and see how close to the edge we were. How close we came to splashing into the cold morning river. Ian tussles my hair and lights a cigarette. He looks bored; eager for the walk home to start his morning shift. I glance at my watch. Five-thirty.

We walk to the bottom of the lane and go our separate ways. The guilt slides in like an unwelcome visitor. I think about Joe and begin to sob, hugging myself as I stumble up the hill towards my childhood home. I miss him so much, I can barely push myself from one day to the next. Killing his unborn baby intensifies the pain to the point where I no longer want to live. I've been lining up paracetamol on the kitchen worktop at 3am every night for the past week.

Ian with his drugs and his passion, just a mobile phone call away, has saved me every time.

I tiptoe up my mother's driveway, hoping my stepdad has already left for work. What a sight I must be, my skirt and bare legs caked in fresh mud. I breathe a sigh of relief when I see his pick-up isn't in the garage. I'm not in the mood for a lecture on morals. I smile when I think he must have driven over the river bridge while Ian and I were down below screwing each other into the ground. I creep up the stairs and hear my mother snoring softly. I decide to risk a shower.

I hold out my hands to catch cupfuls of water, then splash them onto my face. I decide enough's enough. Joe's dead and I've been writhing in exquisite sexual joy with a young druggie on a riverbank. A recent widow should behave with more dignity.

It's mid-afternoon when I wake. Mother's gone to her afternoon job at the hospital. She works in the shop there.

I escape and head for the river. I follow the footpath leading away from the water meadows, up the hill towards the woods. It's here I find the baby's limbs hanging from the lowest branch of a beech tree, or at least that's what they look like in the blistering sunlight. Must be eighty degrees today.

I think about Joe. I want to go to the churchyard and dig him up, just to have his body close to mine again. His bones, the remains of his flesh; it'd be better than nothing.

The insides of my thighs are aching from last night's contortions. I look up at the tree, wishing I had some scissors to cut down the limbs. They're hanging from orange bailer twine. I think about the moles my stepdad used to hang from the trees in the copse down the lane. I remember the thrashing he gave me when I cut them down. I decide to leave these be.

After Joe died I'd go all over our house looking for intimate traces of him. I searched for his pubic hair in the bathroom, inspecting the toilet rim, the bath, the soap; searching for a sign that he'd been there; that he was a part of my life. It seems unbelievable he ever was.

Weeks later I found the ivory blanket with the satin edging. It was covered in his dark brown hair. I spent a whole evening carefully removing each one and putting it into a white envelope lined with cotton wool.

The most amazing find was the Twix bar. I was

searching through the pockets of an old paddock jacket of Joe's when I found it. Half eaten. I looked closely and saw his teeth marks fossilised forever in the caramel and biscuit. I wrapped it up and put it in the freezer. Nobody knows about my mementos.

I sit in the shade of an oak tree and look up at the rooks blackening the blue sky. It's peaceful here; just the sound of the occasional crow scarer in the next field.

It's time to make a decision.

Ian has to go. I'm making a fool of myself; dressing in black, going back to my teenage gothy phase. It's pathetic.

Or is it?

I think about Germaine. She lives in one of the farm cottages at the end of the lane. Okay, so most people call her an old witch behind her back, but now aromatherapy and alternative healing are trendy again, she's in demand. I decide to pay her a visit.

Germaine says she's psychic. I'm sort of hoping she is because I want to get in touch with Joe so badly. He knows the sex is just a release. It's never as real as it was with him.

Soul mates, we used to call each other.

Sometimes when I look in your eyes I can see your soul. We'd sing along, grinning and looking deep into each other's eyes. Same colour. Same look of devotion. Wish I'd still got the James album handy: I'd love to hear that song again, but they persuaded me to put 'our music' away in the loft for now. Just wait till they spot the Twix in the freezer.

Germaine's preparing some herbal remedies for her more gullible clients. They come from the new estate; all company Mondeos and Ikea furniture.

"Took your time to come to me," she says without looking up.

I stare down at my scuffed suede boots against her cracked quarry tiles.

"Suppose you've decided you want to get in touch with him, have you?" Germaine asks, spinning round to face me. Her face is hard, betraying no emotion.

"Not bothered," I shrug and plonk myself down on her rocking chair, pulling a squashy cushion to my chest.

"What you need is more communication with the living, not the dead," she says pulling the cork out of a green bottle. "Elderberry. Made it last year. Bloody strong stuff, this."

She hands me a glass with a bluish tinge; very fashionable.

I sip the ruby liquid cautiously and feel the warmth seep down my gullet. I'm eager for more of the burning sweetness and drink more thirstily this time.

"Steady on. You'll be pissed before you've had chance to pour out your grief, sweetheart," she warns, her voice full of sarcasm.

I smile sheepishly at her. Germaine looks good today. Always velvet; maroon or navy. Always those jet beads. Always those bloody crocheted shawls which make her look like a witch. She hasn't been so heavy-handed on the eyeliner today, and the purple eye-shadow looks great. Her lips have been painted in the usual mulberry shade. They're full and inviting. I gaze with envy at Germaine's full breasts spilling out over the deep 'V' of her velvet bodice. Why can I never quite capture that vampish look of hers?

"Don't suppose you've had any proper counselling since Joe's death?"

Her no-nonsense 'teacher voice' pulls me up short; it's so at odds with her general lack of conformity. Pagan witch, yes. Agony aunt/social worker, definitely not.

I shake my head and look her straight in the eye.

"I've been shagging the arse off Ian, actually."

"Common reaction."

This isn't quite what I expected.

"Sex and death are such close companions," she continues. "I bet it's the best sex you've ever had too? Multiple orgasms, the lot?"

She's broken the ice and we burst out laughing. Germaine refills our glasses.

"So you've come here to get in touch with Joe to see whether he disapproves and whether you should carry on feeling guilty?"

Germaine has adopted her agony aunt pose again.

"Now you put it like that. . ."

Two cats wander in and look at me disinterestedly. I'm now cradling the cushion tighter, gripping the beautiful blue glass and wishing I could stay forever.

"Talk to fifty out of a hundred women in the same boat and they'll tell you they've done exactly the same thing. Shagged themselves stupid."

"I feel so. . . disloyal. I still feel married. I've been unfaithful to Joe, but somehow I feel it serves him right for deserting me." I instantly wish I hadn't said that. The familiar lump plops into my throat and that bastard with the stinging nettle is poking around the backs of my eyes again. I'm determined not to cry in front of Germaine.

"Stop bleating on about disloyalty, for goodness sake, Vanni. Get a grip. This goes much deeper than social convention. You know how religious claptrap was designed to make women feel inferior and guilty. What you're doing is exactly what Nature intended. It's a kind of therapy."

I begin to feel better, yet ashamed that Germaine needed to spell it out to me again. I want to share her beliefs; live my life according to those ancient lores she's always going on about, but . . . I'm afraid.

"I saw the babies again." I take another swig of wine and sink back against the chair.

"Did you ever tell Joe about the abortion?"

I shake my head and close my eyes.

"Don't you see? I've been punished, haven't I? Joe's been taken away from me as punishment. The only man I've ever loved and now this. . ."I begin to sob, letting go of the glass and falling into Germaine's arms.

I AWAKE IN A DOUBLE BED, surrounded by satin cushions and purring cats. Germaine is sitting in the corner by the window, doing some crochet work.

"Not another bloody shawl!"

She turns and smiles.

"Take Ian's comfort, Vanni. You need it."

I sit up and look at her.

"I mean it. He's not a bad lad. Young, impetuous, but he's fond of you. Don't underestimate him."

I think about Ian; his immaturity; his eagerness to please. I wonder if Germaine knows about the drugs.

"Have some fun. To hell with what people think," she says as if reading my thoughts. "Grab the passion and squeeze out every last drop of it. For Goddess's sake, don't feel guilty about it."

I grin at her words. If ever I needed a sister or a mother, then I need look no further.

"You'll be telling me next to move into that battered old caravan with him," I quip, moving aside to let a particularly affectionate cat slope onto my lap.

"If he wasn't my son, I'd say keep well away from that place. Hash City, I call it."

She puts the half-finished shawl to one side and walks towards the bed. "Doesn't do any harm, though, does it? Natural herbal substance. Not as damaging as alcohol."

I think about Joe's tumour and shrug my shoulders.

"Let Ian and I look after you, Vanni."

I sit up and pull my fingers through my hair. "I must look a sight."

Germaine holds out her hand. I take it and as I do so, I feel the guilt edging out of me, blistering through my skin and then it is exposed to the light. I examine it, then try to force it out of the open window. Joe's wicked grin dances before my eyes, and I know it's okay to feel good once in a while.

I look up into Germaine's eyes, but they are closed. She's concentrating hard. I lower my eyes instead to her hands. There are rings on every finger and both thumbs. I kneel down and brush my lips across each one.

ACKNOWLEDGMENTS

My thanks to all those lovely writer friends of mine, who have consistently been generous with their advice, support and encouragement. Thank you, too, to my ever-patient family for letting me just get on with it. I'm very grateful to Jennie Rawlings of Serifim for designing such an amazing cover and to David Penny, who gave me the information I needed to produce a much improved version of this collection.

The Black Queen - Placed 2nd in Round 6 of The Whittaker Prize 2012 with title, Twisted Sheets

    The Fledgling - Placed 1st in the live Write-Invite Competition 28th January 2012

    Smile For The Camera - Joint 5th Place Round 4 of The Whittaker Prize 2012

    Laughing Llamas and A Saxophone - Placed 3rd in The Meridian Summer Competition 2012

    White Sand Cocoon - Placed 3rd in live Write-Invite Competition 13th August 2011, 4th place in Avery Short Story Competition September 2011, Shortlisted in Five Stop

Story January 2012, one of ten shortlisted in The Knock On Effect Competition 2012

Skin and Bone - Placed 1st in the live Write-Invite Competition 24th March 2012

Glam Rock and Scrambled Eggs - Placed 2nd in the live Write-Invite Competition 8th October 2011, Shortlisted 1/32 in The Erewash Writers' Short Story Competition 2012

Alopecia and A Stray Dog - Placed 1st In the live Write-Invite Competition 21st July 2012

Colours Fade To Black and White - As 'Steamed Vegetables' was Shortlisted in The Writers' Forum Competition July/August 2012. Won second prize in The Greenacre Writers Short Story Competition 2013 and published in their anthology.

Helena - First published in *Slipstream* Literary Journal Issue 3 Winter 1997/98.

Surfer Boy - Place 1st in the live Write-Invite Competition 13th October 2012

Twisted Sheets - Published on the website www.100wordstory.org

Camels In A Field - Placed 1st in The Word Hut No. 3 Short Story Writing Competition 2012

Red Meat - Published in Issue 2 of Six Word Story Flash Magazine September 2012

No Oil For Hogmanay - Placed 3rd in The Meridian Short Story Winter Competition 2011/12

Getting It Off Her Chest - Shortlisted in The Wells Literary Festival Competition 2000 and Longlisted in The Fish Short Story Prize 2011/2012

Party Pooper - Specially Commended Certificate in The Ifanca Hélène James Short Story Competition 2012

Broken Bowls and Camel Lashes - Placed 2nd in the live Write-Invite Competition 9th June 2012

Flicking Nails - Shortlisted in Five Stop Story June 2012

Sounds of Darkness - First published on Flash Flood Friday http://flashfloodjournal.blogspot.co.uk/ , 12th October 2012

I Like Your Bow-Ties, Mr Day - Placed 1st in 5 Minute Fiction 1st Birthday Competition, voted for by readers and published on the 5 Minute Fiction Website.

Chaste Kiss Chase - 2nd place in the live Write-Invite Competition November 12th 2011, Honourable Mention in Multi-Story Competition April 2012, Longlisted in The Word Hut Competition No. 5

Black Jacks and Sparrows - Placed 3rd in Round 5 of The Whittaker Prize 2012

Pompeii 1972 - Shortlisted in The Creative Writing Matters Flash Fiction Competition

The Cleansing - Prizewinner in From The Ashes Competition 1999 and published in *Ashes - New Writing* (edited by Alex Keegan)

ABOUT THE AUTHOR

Jo Derrick is the former editor/publisher of both *The Yellow Room Magazine* and *QWF Magazine,* print journals featuring short stories by female writers.

She has been writing professionally since 1990 and has numerous short stories and articles published in a wide range of publications, including *Mslexia, Writers' Forum, Buzzwords, The People's Friend* and *Woman's Weekly Fiction Special.* Many of her short stories and flashes have been successful in competitions, including The Fish Prize and The Bedford International Short Story Competition judged by crime writer, Leigh Russell.

Short stories are Jo's passion, but she has recently completed a psychological crime novel. Her second short story collection (working title Facing The Music) will be published early in 2019.

35009350R00085

Printed in Poland
by Amazon Fulfillment
Poland Sp. z o.o., Wrocław